Brand gets called to Service and waits to meet his Master. He quickly finds out that the Master is a famous football player, Marshall Taylor, but he is undecided about what kind of Servant he wants. Brand is in competition with at least five others and he is put on the spot immediately. He performs well enough to catch the Master's attention, but it is with one of the Master's friends that he makes an immediate connection, Chase McIntyre. Marshall decides to purchase four of the six Servants and moves them into his house. Chase and Brand take their infatuation to a whole new level, leaving them both in a dilemma with no resolution. Chase has to save Brand from some kidnappers, which makes Marshall realize that he should be Brand's true Master. Brand is so close to getting everything he wants, but is it that simple?

This book is a work of fiction. Names, characters, places, and incidents either are products of the author's imagination or are used fictitiously. Any resemblance to actual events or locales or persons, living or dead, is entirely coincidental.

Pick 6 Cages
Copyright © 2021 Crawford Rhine
ISBN: 978-1-4874-3247-8
Cover art by Martine Jardin

Published by eXtasy Books Inc or
Devine Destinies, an imprint of eXtasy Books Inc

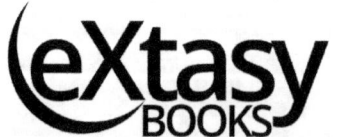

Look for us online at:
www.eXtasybooks.com or www.devinedestinies.com

Pick 6 Cages
The Master & Servant Series 9

By

Crawford Rhine

CHAPTER ONE

My cage was delivered on a hot August day, making me grateful that I was only wearing a very skimpy jock strap. The sweat was rolling down my torso as I sat on the bamboo floor and heard my handlers struggling with placing my cage down in exactly the right spot. The room to which they had delivered me was large, based on the echo of sounds that I could hear. The heavy drape covering the bars of my cage kept me from seeing anything and severely restricted my hearing as well as the air flow.

I had left Charleston a day ago, having been locked inside my cage before I was loaded onto a private jet to be delivered to my Master. It was all by my own choosing, of course. I had waited for this moment for most of my life. In fact, since my thirteenth birthday, I had been waiting and now it was here.

In the hot cage I had nothing to do but wait and think, so I let my mind wander back to my thirteenth birthday party, five years ago. We had a family dinner, like most kids turning my age did. My father, my brothers, and my granddad joined me at our house. My father had made my favorite meal, spaghetti with homemade garlic bread. He had bought me a sheet cake from my favorite local bakery.

There are no women in our world. Females lived on another world, separated from the males. When women had a male baby, they were sent to our side to be raised by the man who had donated the sperm. Sometimes when I was small, I would dream of my Mother, or the representation of the woman who I thought of as her. She was always very kind

1

and very pretty.

Now that I was older, I didn't have those dreams anymore, but just accepted the fact that our worlds were never meant to mix. So my world consisted of men and men who were attracted to men. The majority of our society was NOMARs, or non-marked men. These men were sexually attracted to females, which they were never destined to meet.

A very small percentage of our population was marked men, those that were sexually attracted to males. Marked guys were rare and were revealed to the world on their thirteenth birthday. Different people had different reactions to the revelation of the mark.

My reaction was not one of surprise at the time. I had felt the stirrings inside me before they were confirmed. When my face started to change there at the dinner table, I couldn't see it, but I could see the reaction on the rest of my family's faces. My Dad and Grandfather were worried, my older brother was happy, and my little brother was horrified.

I jumped up from the table and rushed to the hall restroom. Staring into the mirror, I saw the blue line as it developed and expanded along my jaw line. It started as a light spot and then spread from the bottom of my left ear to almost the tip of my chin. The blue of the mark became lighter and brighter before settling on a pale neon hue that remains to this day. I had tried to scrub it off, but it was a part of my skin.

The mark easily identified me as a man who was attracted to other men, which did offer several benefits. One was that I was able to attend a special school, called The Service Academy, or SA, that was run by and only for marked guys. A second benefit to being marked was that after school was over, I would have the chance to enter The Service. The Service was a program that allowed marked guys to enter a fantastic lottery of sorts. The third benefit to being marked was always having a slew of options for sex. Marked guys were fair game, and NOMARs were always willing to fuck.

Wealthy NOMARs used The Service to call for a marked guy to be their sexual Servant. In exchange for this, the NOMAR became a Master and agreed to pay the Servant one million dollars a year for up to two years, according to a contract signed by both parties. If at the end of the first year, the Master wanted to terminate the contract, then the money was paid and the contract was completed.

Most marked guys saw this as a fantastic chance to make a lot of money very quickly. I saw it as a chance to have a fantastic once-in-a-lifetime experience and possibly meet the man of my dreams. Either option—financial well-being or love—made the risk worth it for me. I decided on the spot to enter into The Service when I graduated from the SA.

My two years at the Service Academy had been a blast. I had learned things about sex that I never would have guessed would even be possible. I had also learned a lot about myself. There were things that I did and had done to me that were amazing and I will never forget my time there, ever. Now, however, I was ready for the next chapter of my life, to use all the lessons I had learned to seduce a Master and make him fall in love with me.

I had never really been in love before, although I had crushed on guys hard before. While most of my friends at the SA where digging on each other and fucking nightly in the dorms, I preferred to be more selective and was drawn to some of the older professors and advisors.

My first crush was the dorm advisor who introduced himself to me the first day at the SA. His name was Chip, and he had been a football jock in high school and had gone on to play in college before accepting a contract from a wealthy stockbroker. He had served his two years and now was giving back by working to train new Servants. We had chemistry right away, and I wound up in his bed by the end of the third day. Chip had a great body, but he was a complete bottom that didn't do a thing for me sexually. It was disappointing, but it taught me a valuable lesson about learning to read people better in the future.

My second crush and first full-time relationship came in the form of one of my professors, Dr. Hepskinsky. He was a history professor who was in his mid-forties with the body of a twenty-year-old. He worked out every day, shaved his head and face religiously smooth for class, and had a great sense of humor.

I pursued Hep with all the energy that my sixteen-year-old body gave me. I flirted and I cajoled, plotted and schemed, arranged meetings and hung after class, made office visits and ambushed him in the parking lot. He had no choice but to fuck with me!

Once I got his clothes off, saw his tremendous body and, most importantly, his gigantic lap-hog, there was no way he could stop me from climbing onto him and using him like an adult jungle-gym.

Sex with Hep was eye-opening. His big thick body was covered in thick black hair, in juxtaposition to his head and face. The first time I lay under his massive body and felt his hot cock enter my tiny puckered hole, I thought I had died and gone to heaven. His cock felt like it was splitting me into two, and I held onto his hard biceps as he pushed it all the way inside me.

Hep was a fantastic lover who knew how to fuck. He ripped me a new asshole every time we were together, making sure I was unable to sit down for hours afterwards. His big cock was only overshadowed by his extreme stamina at plowing my sweet hole. I soon came to not be able to do without it, much like being addicted to a drug.

One of the most important things that he did for me was to teach me how to fuck. Sometimes, we would ask Chip to come over with me, and Hep would watch me fuck him, criticizing and complimenting me on the action. On some occasions he would even use his hands to direct my actions, and it wasn't long before my fucking scale scores rocketed to the top of my class. Hep was very proud of me, and I was proud that he saved himself for me alone, never once touching Chip, despite Chip practically begging for him to.

It all came to an end when my Sexual Adviser put the brakes to it. He thought my training needed variety and forbid Hep from fucking with me again. I was devastated, but soon came to see that it was probably for the best. I met several other men at the SA, all older, who I enjoyed spending time with, but never had another man completely dominate me sexually like Hep had done. My time with Hep had been unbelievably transformative, and I would never forget him.

Hep met me in my dorm after graduation on my last day at the SA, and despite the ban against it, he fucked me like a bull fresh into a field of cows, leaving me breathless and sore for days. His graduation present to me was by far my favorite of all of those I had been given.

Hep said that staying away from me was the hardest thing he had ever done and he hoped I would come back after my calling to work at the SA, so we could be together. It was a flattering proposal, but I knew that I had many adventures yet to come before I could even think about that step.

The Service Academy had prepared me for a lot of things, but to receive that phone call from The Service was life-altering. It was almost the end of August when I was called. The Service had called me on a Monday and expected me to be ready to go on a Friday.

I entered the cage on Friday morning, after stripping my clothes off and putting on a neon green jock strap that was basically little more than a half-washcloth-size piece of fabric in the front that was supported by three bands of elastic. My whole ass was exposed.

My cage had been built according to my unique body spec-
ifications. I was six-foot-one, so my cage was tall, not enough
for me to stand up in, but big enough to squat on my toes and
not have to dip my head. Bamboo floors and polished steel
bars completed the cage, along with a door and a padlock in
the front. The heavy drapes were gathered in the back, but
would be pulled around the cage once I entered.

Crawling into the cage, I was surprised to see that hanging
on the back bars were a giant hamster-like water bottle and
an empty container, in which I guessed I was supposed to use
the bathroom. The cage was spacious, but terrifying none the
less. The drape was pulled around the bars of my cage, cutting off my vision and muffling most but the loudest of noises.
It completed my feelings of helplessness and submissiveness.
I was an independent person, and the fact that I was going to
completely submit myself to someone else was very foreign
to me, but I had already told myself to commit to it. My scores
at the SA in the area of taking direction and submitting to au-
thority were always poor.

I sat cross-legged on the smooth floor and listened intently,
trying to tell what was happening. I heard the sound of the
forklift as it skewered my cage and lifted it into the hold of
the jet. As far as I knew, I was the only passenger besides my
handlers, so there should have been plenty of room. The plane
took off and travelled for more than an hour and a half, if my
sense of time in a darkened room was any good. From
Charleston, that meant that we were either still on the East
Coast or in the eastern section of the Mid-West.

When the plane finally landed, the forklift deposited my
cage into the back of some type of truck. From the halting advance of the truck, I guessed we were somewhere with a lot
of traffic. Sometimes I could hear car horns beeping angrily.
The back of the truck was very warm, and soon I was

drenched in sweat. This was ruining all the primping I had done in anticipation of meeting my Master. Finally, the truck came to a stop and I was unloaded.

Now back in the here and now, I was still waiting in my cage where it had been finally placed. I heard the handlers arrive again and the sound of the same dolly that had brought me into the room. And then the unmistakable sound of another cage being lowered into place right beside me drifted into my cage.

What the fuck is going on? Why would there be another cage?

I was so tempted to look out of the drapes or to call out.

Why would there be another cage being delivered? Can a Master have more than one Servant?

After giving it a second thought, I saw that the answer to that question would be in the affirmative, but it had never occurred to me before. I had put all of my energy and devotion into the hope of winning over this mysterious Master and I didn't think I would like having competition at all. In fact, I knew I would not like it.

I was still pondering the situation when another cage was delivered. This one wasn't as close to me as the last, but I could definitely hear it and knew what the sounds meant. Now my head was really spinning. I waited impatiently for the sound of another cage being delivered, but none came. There was a long period of silence in which I tried hard to hear the other Servants in their cages making noise. They obviously were also listening and none of us made even so much as a cough.

The air conditioning in the room had cooled me off, but now my sweat had dried on the surface of my skin, giving me a gross feeling that nothing but a shower would cure. The air was also making my nipples hard enough to cut glass. This was not the way I had wanted to meet my Master, but I had little choice about it now.

Suddenly a door opened in the distance and there were

clicking sounds of heels on hardwood floors. This room must have been very large, because it took the man a little while to cross it or even to get to the middle of it, from the sounds. When he did, the footsteps stopped, and I heard him clear his throat.

"Servants, if I could have your attention!" His voice was clear and controlled.

I found myself to be fascinated by these events, but at the same time, I felt that I was completely out of control with what was happening and couldn't wait to see what was next.

"I'm a representative from The Service, and today is a very special day. We have a very important Master-in-the-making and he has chosen a very old method of calling his Servants, one that is not done often. You have been chosen to be a part of a very unusual call process referred to as a Pick Six!"

CHAPTER TWO

If I had thought that I was confused before, it was nothing compared to how I felt now. What the hell was a Pick Six, and why had we never been taught about it in school?

The speaker's voice continued. "Today, you have been called for a very special ceremony. When a new Master is undecided about what he would like, he can ask for a sample of Servants to . . . interview. This is called a Pick Six."

A sample? So the Master gets to look us over, fuck us, and then pick one? We're in a fucking contest for him? And there are six of us? Well, bring it! I'm ready!

"You do not have a contract yet, so therefore the Master cannot demand anything from you sexually. At the end of this session, one of you will have a contract or all of you will be returning home."

The gravity of it all hit me like a ton of bricks. This could be my calling, but also could mean that I was going back home empty-handed. The guy from The Service had said that the Master could not demand anything from us sexually, but I bet if we didn't fuck with him, he would not pick us. I wondered if we could be the aggressor in this instance. My mind was going a million miles-an-hour.

The representative from The Service continued. "My advice to you is to make a good impression. The sex is implied, so don't be overly aggressive or attention-seeking or it will come off as desperate."

That answers that.

I had already formed a game-plan for the first time I met my Master in my head, but now all of that was out of the window. Now I had to compete for his attention without coming off too strong. I was in trouble, because strong was my specialty.

"I wish you luck, and I will be here at the end to help one of you sign your contract into The Service." And with that, he was gone. I heard his heels clicking across the hardwoods and the opening and closing of a door on the opposite side of the room.

I sat there in silence, listening intently. It felt like a long time, but I was not a patient guy, so I was a really poor judge of how much time had elapsed. Soon there was the sound of the door opening again, and a wall of sound hit my cage.

It was men, there was no doubt about that, and from the sounds of them, a big group. As they drew closer to us, I could make out whistles and laughter. I guessed that this Master must have brought friends with him to help him pick which of us marked guys would be a good Servant for him. I smiled to myself as I pictured it, the wealthy NOMAR version of window shopping.

I realized that I was holding my breath, so I practiced some deep breathing I had been taught at the SA and rose up into The Service Squat position. The Service Squat was the acceptable position for all Servants to take when meeting their Masters or when they were unsure of what to do. It was like a temporary position to fall back into when a situation was unclear.

The Squat consisted of being up on the balls of your feet with your thighs spread wide open and your head bowed. Your arms were supposed to be on top of your thighs, following the V shape that they made. It was a position that hurt at first, but after years of practice, it now seemed very natural to me. I looked forward to the moment when I could stand normally though, despite my comfort with it.

The men suddenly stopped talking and horsing around

,and the room got quiet. A voice rang out. "Good morning, marked men!"

There was a slight echo in the room, telling me that this room was bigger than I had imagined it in my head.

"I'm a Master in need of a Servant, and hopefully one of you in here is going to blow me away and be that man for me today."

His words made my blood boil with heat. I was so ready to have a Master that I knew I was going to come off as desperate unless I kept myself under control and focused on the task at hand. His voice was deep and confident, and I knew that he would make a good Master from just hearing it.

The Master's voice continued. "I'm very excited to meet each one of you today, and I brought my boys along to help me decide, so if you guys are ready, so are we!" The group of NOMARs yelled and cheered.

I couldn't hear anything else for a minute until I heard a ripping sound to my right and then footsteps around my cage. Suddenly bright sunlight came streaming onto me as I realized that my drape was being pulled back. The light was blinding, and I quickly blinked my eyes, trying to adjust.

Then the sound of the drapes being pulled open on the cage to my left came to my ears. I stole a furtive glance sideways and saw a cage on each side of me, separated from me by six feet or so. The wood flooring of the room was parquet, and it came to me that we were in some kind of a ballroom or basketball court.

The next sound that I heard was of the padlock being unlocked and removed from the cage to my right, then from mine, and then from the one to my left. I quickly looked over into the cage to my right, seeing a skinny white guy with blond hair brushed into his eyes, a la Justin Bieber. He was looking at me also, so I smiled slightly and subtly looked to my left. This cage held an Asian guy who was very short but

11

beautifully built, with his head shaved into a flattop. His cage was a lot smaller than mine, since each one was custom built to our height.

The Master's voice rang out again. "You may exit your cages, marked men."

I noticed that he was going out of his way to avoid calling us Servants yet, since only one of us was going to get the title. I lowered myself out of The Service Squat and onto all fours. This was the moment that I had been waiting for that was more than three years in the making—the moment where I would meet my Master face to face . . . maybe.

I pushed open the cage door and, just as I had been taught, took two hand steps forward and rose back into The Squat. I kept my head lowered the whole time, but glanced sideways enough to see that there were more than just the three of us that I had been able to see from my cage.

"Fucking fantastic!" one of the NOMARs said, excitedly. It didn't sound like the Master's voice.

"Glorious, isn't it?" This was the Master.

I was excited that I could already tell his voice apart from others in a crowd.

"Fucking A!"

"Very good, fellas. Now, I'm going to come to each one of the six of you, one at a time. When I speak to you, you may look up and answer me. Is that clear?"

All of us knew to answer when asked a direct question, so there were six voices in unison saying, "Yes, sir." The Pick Six was a true pick of six marked men. I was amazed at the influence and power the Master must have had in order to get this special treatment. I didn't think that your average millionaire would be granted this option, but didn't really know for sure.

I heard the crowd of NOMARs move to my far right. I still didn't know where I was in the line of Servants-to-be, but I would be finding out shortly. I was grateful that I did not have to go first. The Master kept his voice low, and the only thing I heard from that first interview was the murmur of approval that went up from the Master's posse at the end of it.

I was instantly jealous of the first Servant and the positive sounds that I heard from the group of NOMARs. Telling myself to snap out of it, I concentrated on how I wanted myself to be perceived.

The shuffling feet sound told me that the crowd had moved down to the second Servant. I could make out a few words now, but not a complete sentence. I was amazed at how long the Master was staying with each applicant, more because it had just popped into my head that I was going to be in this Service Squat for a very long time.

The moving crowd told me that Master was now interviewing the Servant in cage number three, and this was the cage right beside me to the left. I was next! My heart started pumping and the burn in my thighs intensified.

"What is your name?"

"Robert, sir."

"Where are you from, Robert?"

"Minnesota, sir."

"Vikings fan?"

"What, sir?" This Servant, liked most marked men that I had met, was not a sports fan. He didn't know how to answer.

"Are you a fan of the Minnesota Vikings football team?" Master spelled it out with relaxed ease.

"My family is. I don't really watch football."

The boys let out a chorus of *oohs* at that, sounding vaguely disappointed, and I mentally told myself to be prepared if they were football players or big sports fans.

"And what would your hobbies be, then?"

"I like to cook and I'm really good at cleaning."

The Master was very contemplative when he said, "Well, that certainly could come in useful."

"Yes, sir."

"Well, thank you. We're going to move on now."

The Servant had the good sense to know to stay quiet, and out of the corner of my eye, I saw him bow his head again. The mass of men moved in front of me.

"You may look up." The Master's voice was even more firm and direct now that it was aimed at me.

I looked up and saw an amazing group of guys. I recognized the Master immediately, and I instantly felt relief because I knew what to do next. I tried to keep my face as neutral as possible, but I was a little star struck.

The Master seemed surprised by my reaction and said, "Do you know who we are?"

I focused my eyes on his and told myself not to look away. "Yes, sir." Having lived with a bunch of marked guys at the SA, I discovered that my love of almost all sports was a rarity. It was more of a NOMAR trait than a marked man trait, and it really separated me from the pack. I was now going to use it to my full advantage.

"Who?" He sounded frustrated. At The Service Academy, we had been warned that a common new Master mistake was not being direct enough with us. Unless we were asked a question, we were not allowed to say anything. This sometimes frustrated new Masters who were not used to being so direct or so commanding.

"Well, you are Marshall Taylor, and these are some Colossals," I said proudly. Marshall was the quarterback for the New York Colossals and was one of three brothers playing in the NFL. His Dad was also an NFL legend. He had a boyish charm about him, but not the kind of guy I had always pictured as my Master. There was not much about him that turned me on, sexually, but I was sure that I could make him happy, regardless of that.

I recognized some of the other faces around him, but I did

not know their names. Besides Marshall, there were six other guys with him, although I could only see the faces of five of them.

"Oh fuck, Marshall! You found a sports fan!" The voice drew my eyes to the speaker, who stepped out from behind Marshall, giving me my first glance of Chase McIntyre.

He was one of my favorite players, mostly because he was so fucking hot—the kind of hot that just smolders. He was dark and muscular, with a fire that was burning right under his skin. My mouth formed the word *Chase* before I could even stop myself. He was one of the sexiest men I had ever seen, and I could not believe that I was standing in front of him now.

"Looks like he knows you too, Chase!" Marshall said, starting to laugh, which caused the other guys to chuckle and slap Chase on the back.

One of the other guys laughed. "Chase is a real ass-hound, so I'm sure he will know him later if he doesn't now."

"He does love fucking that ass," another one said.

Master turned back to me and said, "What's your name?"

"Brand, sir."

"Brand." He let the name hang there on his lips. "That's a cool name, and you're tall, based on your cage. How tall?"

"Over six-foot-one, sir."

He shook his head. "Where are you from?"

"Charleston, sir."

"I love Charleston. You're right in the middle of a bunch of teams there. Who's your favorite?"

I took a second to steal a glance at Chase, who was intently watching me. "I'm a Steelers fan, Master."

The boys all smirked at that, and I enjoyed that I had surprised some of them with my pick.

"But I'm an even bigger Tarheel fan, sir."

"College football? Hakeem will love that!" Marshall said to

his friends. He had turned to face them, so I was able to stare at Chase McIntyre some more. He was shorter than most of the other guys, but was broad and dark and mysterious. My crotch tingled at the sight of his dark brooding eyes and his thick muscular neck and body.

"Anything else, Tarheel fan?" Master's question had surprised me and I jerked my attention away from Chase McIntyre and back to Marshall. I still couldn't believe that I was in the presence of these famous jocks and that there was a possibility by the end of the afternoon that I would belong to Marshall Taylor.

I started to speak and then hesitated, wondering whether I should or not.

He prompted me. "Go on . . ."

"I was just thinking how a Pick Six isn't usually so lucky for someone in your position, sir. I hope this one goes better for you than usual." In football terms, a Pick Six is when the quarterback throws an interception and the opposing team runs it back for a touchdown, which is worth six points. Marshall was a quarterback, and a Pick Six would be the worst thing that could have happened to him in a game.

All of the NOMARs burst into laughter, slapping Marshall on the back and high-fiving each other. I couldn't take my eyes off of Chase McIntyre, and he seemed to not be able to look at anything but me.

"Smart ass!" Marshall spit out at me, even though he was laughing. "I certainly hope that this Pick Six is good for me, as well." He looked at me with his head cocked to the side for a minute, like he was watching an animal to see what it would do next.

"I like the smart mouth on this one!" Marshall noted out loud to himself. "We are moving on. Thank you, Brand."

"Welcome, Master," I said, bowing my head and smiling to myself. I was glad I'd referred to him with his title.

CHAPTER THREE

I felt like that had gone as well for me as it could have. Master was a celebrity and a sports figure, so it was very exciting. I reviewed my conversation with the boys again in my head as I squatted there in the middle of that ballroom. I don't think there was one single word or action I would have done differently.

The only face I could picture when I closed my eyes was the Master's friend, Chase McIntyre. If I got the chance to fuck with him, I think my ass and eyes might explode with pleasure. It would be a dream-come-fucking-true! I tried to listen to the marked guy on my left answering Master's questions, but my mind wandered right back to my interview.

Marshall seemed to be a really nice person. I got a good feeling about him, even from the little bit of time we had spent together. His friends seemed nice, and I was overjoyed to even have a chance at this. My Dad would be shitting his pants right now if he knew that I had just met these two famous footballers.

Before I even realized it, the interviews were over and my heart started racing at what would happen next. The group of NOMARs moved back to the middle of the room, so they were sort of in front of me. I saw that most of the Servants were watching what was going on, so I didn't feel the need to bow my head any longer. I could feel Chase McIntyre's gaze on me, and my cock hardened.

Marshall Taylor took a step forward and addressed us as a group. "Marked men, I want to thank you for your time and your patience. I enjoyed talking to each of you."

Master's voice sounded sincere, and I felt that he was.

The far door opened as the representative from The Service entered. He walked up to Marshall and his boys and had a quick conversation. There was a lot of head shaking and talking amongst all the parties. Some of the boys were pointing, but none of them at me. I didn't know whether that was good or bad, but knew there was nothing I could do about it.

The Service Rep spoke now to us. "Gentlemen, Mr. Taylor has not made his final decision yet, but he has made the first cut. Denny and Robert, I'm sorry but you have not been selected. Please walk to the open door, and my assistant will show you where to go."

Robert, beside me, stood up on shaky legs and walked forward. He turned briefly towards me, grimacing, and I tried to give him a sympathetic smile. Denny was number six, way down the line, so I never even saw what he looked like. Now I had a one in four chance of becoming Marshall's Servant and my head spun with the implications.

"Mr. Taylor would like one more walk-through. You may stand for this round." The Service Rep didn't seem pleased by this, but he was trying his best to make his client happy.

Marshall and the boys took one more trip down the front of us. I was extremely happy to be able to stand and took advantage of that fact by stretching and shaking my legs out while I waited. I could not hear the questions being asked or the answers this time, and when the party moved in front of me, I concentrated on pictures of dead puppies. I hoped this would stop my hard pole from sticking out of the top of the fabric basket of my jock.

It didn't work. My cock was longer than average, and it was now poking up through the mesh fabric. Most, if not all, of the guys noticed and snickered about it as they stood in front of me.

"Brand . . ." Marshall said.

I knew not to say anything when there wasn't a question posed, but I was extremely happy that he had remembered my name.

"What sexual position are you the best at?"

I took a pause while I made eye contact with Chase McIntyre. "Now, Master, that's like me asking you which one of your pass plays you are the best at. Why would I name one when I'm really good at all of them?"

The entire group burst out laughing. Marshall stopped laughing and regarded me with a shrewd eye. "I've read your file, Brand. I know which one you are the best at . . ."

"And the scouts thought they had you pegged when you first started, Master, but you proved them wrong with not one Super Bowl ring, but two."

"Well, played, Brand." Master smirked at me.

"I promise you, Master, you won't be disappointed!" I said, grinning and catching Chase's eyes before turning them back to Marshall.

"I hope not." He smirked as he moved down the line to the last Servant.

I stood and tried not to be too happy with myself. Still afraid of being crushed by Taylor not picking me, I tried to prepare myself for bad news, just in case.

The group finally went back to the middle of the ballroom and discussed things with The Service Rep. There was a lot of head shaking and talking. Finally, Marshall moved forward and addressed us.

"I have enjoyed meeting all of you and I'm having a really hard time deciding, so I've decided to keep you all."

A ripple ran through the crowd, and I saw the disgusted look on The Service Rep's face. I was thrilled! At least this way, I was guaranteed a contract. My Dad would be so proud, and my year was going to be very exciting at the side of a professional athlete.

"Marshall, that's four million dollars!" one of his friends said, incredulous.

"Yeah, so? My brother has two Servants, why can't I do him two better?"

"Fuck, are you sure?"

"I'm pretty sure."

The Service Rep finally said, "Well then, are you ready to sign four contracts, Mr. Taylor?"

"I think I am!"

CHAPTER FOUR

A fter several hours of paperwork, I was back in my cage, heading to my new Master's house. All four of us were now his Servants, and he unlocked all of our cages at the same time again, this time in his bedroom.

I had rarely even considered being with another Servant when I was called to Service, let alone with three other Servants, all brand new. It was going to be a challenge and an exciting adventure, that was for sure.

"I'm going to give you guys a chance to get to know each other while I set the guys up downstairs watching the Yankees. I'll be right back." Master seemed nervous now that he had four of us hanging on his every word and waiting to fulfill his every sexual desire.

Marshall left the room, and the four of us looked at each other. I held out my hand to the guy beside me and said, "Hi, I'm Brand from South Carolina."

He shook hands with me and said, "I'm Braden from Jersey." He was a nice looking black guy, young and muscled. But he had to be at least eighteen years old, because the Service didn't call anyone younger than that.

The other two had moved close to Braden and me now. The third one of us looked like he was probably a wrestler. He had a thick neck, short and stocky with small ears and shaggy brown hair. He held out a thick, calloused hand and said, "I'm Jeremy from Iowa." Jeremy was probably in his very early twenties.

"Brand."

The last guy was the Asian-American, who introduced himself as *Alex from Florida*. Alex had that look that made it really hard to tell how old he was. My guess was either eighteen or nineteen.

"Can you believe that he called for four of us?" I asked, breaking the ice.

"Fuck, no," Jeremy said. "I didn't even know you could do that."

"So, the four of us are supposed to satisfy this one man?" Alex asked.

"I guess."

"At least you knew who he was," Braden said, looking chagrined.

"Hey, we all got picked, so we all had something he liked," I said, spinning it to the positive.

Alex asked, "What did you guys answer to the question about sex? We could use that information in a few minutes."

"I said my specialty was blowjobs," Braden admitted.

Jeremy added, "I told him that I ride a mean cock."

They all looked at me, and I shrugged my shoulders slightly and said, "I wouldn't tell him, because I do it all well." The guys laughed and said I was ballsy.

Alex admitted that he liked to be fucked hard, but being fisted was his thing.

"You think we're going to have to satisfy the boys after we finish with Marshall?" I asked.

"For sure," was the consensus.

"Can you imagine thinking you got called to Service and then not making the cut like those two poor guys with us?" I asked next.

"How awful would that be to have to go back home now and wait again?" Braden commented.

"Devastating," Alex agreed.

"I hope you guys aren't into drama, because I'm hoping for

a fun year of getting fucked, seeing the world, and making some money," Jeremy said, staring to laugh.

"Cheers to that!" I hooted.

"Looks like it is going to be fun."

"Let's have a blast!" We were all laughing when our Master walked back into the big bedroom.

"Well, I'm glad to see that you guys are getting along," Master said, entering the room. His face was flushed, and I wondered if his boys had been busting his balls downstairs about what was to come next.

The four of us had dropped down silently into The Service Squat, waiting for directions. Marshall seemed nervous for the first time and hesitated a little too long. I felt badly for him and decided to take matters into my own hands, at least for the moment.

Reaching up to my hips, I hooked my thumbs into the jock strap's elastic bands and pushed my neon green undergarment to the floor. Marshall's eyes were immediately on me as I stepped out of the jock and towards him.

"Master, would you like us to undress you now?"

He swallowed hard and said, "Yes."

My comrades in arms immediately snapped into action, pushing their jocks to the floor and helping me with Marshall's suit. I pulled his jacket off, loving how the expensive fabric felt, and handed it off to Alex, who was holding a suit hanger in his hand. Jeremy was kneeling in front of our Master, unbuckling his belt and unfastening his pants. Braden was already untying Master's shoes and pulling his socks off. I could tell that this Service thing was going to be a whole lot easier and faster with four of us than with one.

When Master was standing with nothing but his boxers on, Jeremy had planted his mouth on the thin fabric and was blowing big bursts of hot air into his crotch. I watched as Master's eyes fluttered and he tilted his head back, letting one big hand come to rest on Jeremy's bushy hair. That was the last moment of peace that Master received in the next half-hour. The four of us were focused on him like nothing I had ever seen before.

Alex pushed Master's boxers down from his hips, and Marshall's big tool sprang forward. His cock was already hard and stuck straight out from his golden-haired crotch like an arrow. It was a really good dick. Master had a weapon of mass destruction that was beautiful to behold. It was longer than average, with substantial girth, and straight and level. The head was raised up on the top of the shaft and flush with the bottom of it, giving me the impression of a barbed spear—just the sort of tool you would use if you were standing in a river and needed to spear a passing fish for your dinner. I was impressed.

Alex and I both dropped to our knees to home in on the action of blowing our new Master. Jeremy had the front row seat, so he was the first to swallow Marshall's big monster. Braden was sucking on Master's little ball sack and Alex stood up to lick and suck his nipples. Master didn't know what or who to touch next as he let his hands roam from one of our heads to the next.

I had fought Jeremy for a few licks on Master's cock-sickle, but was mostly shut out, so I moved behind him, knelt at his ass, and began to rim him. Now, Master truly was in a bind, because if he moved forward to escape my relentless tongue, he drove his cock further into Jeremy's hot mouth. If he pulled back from Jeremy's suck-hole, he got the tip of my tongue penetrating his hot ass. Master bucked and flailed under our attention.

Marshall finally took charge, pulling his cock out of Jeremy's mouth and into Alex's open hole. We all switched places and I got to suck on Master's nipples. His chest was mostly smooth, with occasional blondish hairs cropping up.

His nipples were soft and hardened easily under my sandy tongue. He had a great taste, musky and salty. I really enjoyed his smell, as well. His smell reminded me a little of a campfire, although I could tell it was some type of expensive cologne mixed with his musky natural odor.

"Oh, fuck, me!" Master moaned, being carried away by all four or us. He pulled his wet member out of Alex's vortex of a mouth and stuffed it into Braden. I could barely wait until it was my turn to suck on that beautiful joint.

I moved down onto my knees again, starting to roll his hard little balls around in my mouth and licking his grundle while holding his sack against his thigh. I was just starting to enjoy myself when Master shifted positions and pushed his cockhead against my lips. I opened wide and pushed my face into his crotch, swallowing his big tool. I almost gagged at its length, but was able to pull back just in time not to embarrass myself.

Marshall Taylor tasted delicious, and I couldn't get enough of his hot cock in my mouth. I saw the look of jealousy in Jeremy's eyes when Master grabbed my head with both hands and pumped his hips forward, face-fucking me until he came.

Master roared with his climax. "Holy sssshhhhhiiiiiitttttt!"

His cum was nutty and thick and I swallowed the first part of it just to keep myself from choking. Jeremy put a big hand around Master's shaft and milked more of it into my mouth. I let Master's cum fill my mouth and then pulled off of him. Looking up to make sure he was watching me, I let the cum flow a little out of my mouth before leaning over and kissing Jeremy in a full French lip-lock. Jeremy immediately started to snake Master's sweet cream from my mouth with his greedy tongue. I stood up and shared with Alex and Braden, as well, before swallowing the rest down my gullet.

"Goddamn." Master moaned, his eyes never leaving my face. "Brand, why didn't you tell me you were such a fantastic cocksucker?"

"That's only because the other three primed the pump for me, Master. You read my file. My ass is even better than my mouth."

Marshall's eyes seemed to glaze over as he stood there. Finally, he snapped himself out of it and said, "Kneel here in front of me in a line."

I did love when he commanded us. We followed his direction and sat back on our heels, waiting for the next set of commands.

"That was unbelievable, boys." He took a breath and looked down at us fondly. "But I don't think I can fuck under that kind of pressure, not yet."

What does that mean? I couldn't tell where he was going with this.

"I'm going to fuck Jeremy and Braden for now. Brand, I know that Chase is dying to get between your legs, so I was thinking you should go downstairs and see if he wants to spend a little time with you while I'm busy."

I couldn't keep the grin off my face—and Master noticed.

"Well, I can see you are up for that," he said, pointing at my cock that was hard as a rock once more and bouncing at his great news.

"Yes, sir, unless you need me here," I said, praying it wasn't the case.

"No, go on."

As I headed for the door, I heard Master ask Alex if he thought he could handle the four other boys by himself. Alex's enthusiastic "Yes!" was the last thing I heard before closing the door.

I had no idea where I was in this house, but I remembered Master saying that the boys were downstairs and I could hear some kind of noise coming from the right, so I went in that direction. I immediately regretted not grabbing my jock strap off of the floor before leaving.

Soon I found a staircase that led to the first floor. This house was gorgeous and huge. The voices were louder now, and I walked through a kitchen that looked like it should have been on the cover of a home improvement magazine before finding another set of stairs going to another floor. The boys' voices were streaming up the staircase, so I knew I needed to go down one more level.

The stairs brought me right down into a man-cave. In front of me was a huge leather sectional full of men. They were watching the baseball game on the biggest TV I had ever seen. The smell of beer was strong, and I had spotted the top of Chase McIntyre's head almost immediately.

I stopped in place for a few seconds, trying to figure out what the best way to get his attention would be. Deciding to approach him from behind, I walked up to the giant couch and leaned over the top cushion beside his head. I reached down, touched him on his shoulder and softly said, "Sir."

Chase McIntyre immediately grabbed my wrist and jerked his head towards me. His brow was knit with concern until he recognized me, asking, "Brand?"

"Yes, sir." I felt his grip relax and someone paused the game.

"Come around here so we can get a look at you." His voice was deep and absolute.

My already-hard cock throbbed at how his voice attempted to command me. "Sir?" The last thing I wanted to do was stand naked in front of a bunch of horny, possibly drunk NOMARs. I was extremely aware that I now had all of Master's friends' attention.

His tone immediately dropped an octave and his brow seemed to protrude over his eyes even more than usual, as he said, "You heard me. Get your ass over here. Don't make me tell you again."

I didn't say anything else, but took off. I rounded the sectional and moved in front of the giant TV screen. Most of the guys were reclining on parts of the couch that extended, and all of them were drinking. I felt all five gazes on my naked body as I walked. I stopped right in front of Chase, which was also the middle of the room. When he commanded me, I felt something inside that I had never felt before.

"That's more like it." His light gray eyes sparkled with joy at either the sight of me naked in front of him or his command of me. The rest of the boys chuckled at my obvious discomfort.

My crotch-rocket was so hard that it was pointed straight up against my belly and was threatening to blast off if he continued to stare at me.

"I can see that you are excited to see me," he said with a smirk. "What can I do for you, Brand?"

"Master Marshall has found himself busier than he expected and wondered if you might like my company until he needs me again, sir."

"How much do I love that fucking man? Marshall Taylor is the man!" he yelled. A huge smirk spread over the side of his face, as he turned back to me. "Those were his exact words, young one?"

I decided to fight back a little and said, "No, his exact words were, *Tell Chase to fuck you first with his little dick so that you'll be ready for Daddy's big monster afterwards.*"

The entire group burst out laughing. Some of the boys were laughing so hard they rolled over on the couch and pounded the leather.

Chase's smirk turned into a full-fledged grin. "Come here!" He pointed to the floor beside him.

I didn't want to, but I followed his order. I was drawn to him and afraid of him at the same time, like you would be with a beautiful exotic cat. Chase McIntyre was my beautiful black panther, deadly and desirable at the same time.

He sat up, closing the recliner part of the couch where he was sitting. "Lean over my legs."

Oh, fuck! He's going to spank me!

I resigned myself to it with one last look into his gorgeous face to see if he was serious. He was. I lay across his legs, my hard-on pressed uncomfortably against his hairy thighs. Touching him was similar to being electrocuted, as far as I was concerned. Every nerve ending in my skin was going bonkers. My eyes were full of him and I couldn't believe how good he smelled when I was near him. His smell was a mixture of cigars and sweat . . . pure man.

"Your cock is pressed against me like it's in a Panini machine," Chase said.

I knew not to say anything.

"I'm going to spank you for that little comment you made over there and I'm not going to stop until you come. Do you understand?"

"Yes, sir," I said, hanging my head over his legs.

"Don't fret, Brand. You're going to get a little bit of pleasure with your pain today."

I stayed quiet, picturing the smirk on his face. His big rough hand came down flat on my ass, pushing me forward onto his legs. It hurt, but not as bad as I thought it would. I could feel my cock start to shrink, since my mind was on my burning ass, and I immediately squeezed my eyes shut and tried to picture this man on top of me, fucking the shit out of me.

My visualization worked, and between that and the friction created when his hand pushed me forward, I was able to remain hard, and by the seventh or eighth whack, I was ready to climax.

"I'm coming, sir," I said quietly.

My words halted his hand and he said, "What?"

"I'm coming, sir," I repeated.

"Stand and show us."

Just to further humiliate me, as I stood up, I saw Alex had entered the room. Chase touched my red-hot cock with his hand, made hot by the spanks, and that was all I needed to fall over the edge of my climax. My back arched, my head was thrown back, my hips thrust forward, and my cock shot the most beautiful arcs of hot spunk into the air.

Chase McIntyre moved his legs just in time, avoiding being splashed. He watched my cock intently, his grin spreading bigger and bigger.

"Excellent! Now I'm going to go and fucking tear up that tight little hole of yours." He started to laugh.

"What about the rest of us?" one of the others asked.

"I'm here for the rest of you, sir," Alex said, coming forward right on cue.

"Happy fucking, boys!" Chase smiled as he stood up, impressing me with his stature, even though he was just an inch taller than me. "I know I'm going to be occupied for a while."

And with that, he stepped over the pool of cum on the rug, grabbed my hand, and pulled me after him.

CHAPTER FIVE

I followed Chase McIntyre upstairs, my body so full of nervous energy that it was practically ringing like a bell. He led me up to the second floor and down the hallway. I could hear the moaning coming from Master's bedroom as we passed by it, and I was glad that they were having a good time.

Chase stopped in front of a door, turned around, and said, "Marshall lets me use this room when I stay over." His round face was set in a determined gaze. His black five o'clock shadow was thick, framing his face nicely.

I nodded my head to show that I heard him. He raised a big, meaty, rough hand up to my face, palming my jaw-line. He moved his thick thumb over my cheek slowly. His beautiful eyes held mine in a gaze like a laser lock. His lips opened, and then he said, "I'm going to give you a fucking like you've never had before."

"Not before I give you the same thing, sir."

He grinned broadly, his eyes hooded under his protruding eyebrows, barely visible. "Your smart mouth is going to be your undoing . . ." Chase's giant tanned biceps flexed as he hit his fist into his palm.

"I guess I'm going to get undone a lot then, sir," I said with a smirk.

He flung open the door and pushed me through. Closing it behind him, he turned to me as I knelt on the thick carpet. He kicked his dress shoes off and walked over to where I was kneeling. I immediately reached up and ran my hands over his torso. Chase was so freaking ripped and thickly-muscled

31

in every part of his body. He lifted his dress shirt off over his head as I undid his belt and dress pants.

His chest was unnaturally hot. His muscles were all defined, and his sweet little pink nipples stood out from his tan skin, hanging off the edge of his pecs. His abs led all the way down to his hips where his Adonis belt made a *V* shape that curved right down inside his pants to his crotch. His dark hair formed an umbrella over the top of his chest with just a thin line that ran down the middle of his chest and to the top of his belly button.

I licked my lips as I stared at him. He was so close to me now that my nose was full of his smell and every nerve in my body was on edge. Pushing his pants down to the thick carpet, I saw that he was wearing boxer briefs. The sight of him standing there naked except for the stark white briefs was almost more than I could take. Turning my attention to his feet, I slowly took his dress socks off of his feet, noticing that they were tan like the rest of him.

Chase McIntyre's feet were stunning. I expected them to be big, flat, and uncared for, but on the contrary, they were well-cared-for and very sexy. Each of his toes was squared off and thick with a very light smattering of black hair on some of them.

He must have noticed me staring, because he said, "Do you like my feet, young one?"

"Yes, sir." I smiled shyly up to him.

"Good, because you are going to be sucking on them later."

I licked my lips and said, "Yes, sir!"

"Brand, I think we are going to get along very well."

"I won't know that until I see your cock, sir." I smirked, placing my nose against the fabric of his boxer briefs and inhaling deeply. His musky feral smell filled my senses, driving me out of my mind.

"You little fuck! You're gonna see my cock right now."

With one hand, Chase held my neck in a vise-grip, and with the other he pushed his boxer-briefs down, revealing his substantial cock.

My eyes widened noticeably. It was a huge cock! Long and thick, with big veins that stood out from the flesh, this tool had everything that I loved in a cock. The head was larger than the shaft, sitting on top of it like a ripe apple on a thick branch. The whole dong was a work of art, beautifully arching out of a black nest of wiry hair.

"Holy fuck! No wonder you didn't get all that mad when I said that you had a little cock in front of the other guys." I knew that I was star-struck, seeing a professional athlete that I had lusted after on TV, but everything about him was perfect for me, so far. I liked his personality, I loved the hot things he threatened me with, I could not get enough of his body, and now his cock was staring at me, begging to be sucked.

"You like it, young one?"

I grabbed the root of his cock with a hand and said, "I love it, sir."

I lunged for him with an open mouth, engulfing him with my hot tongue and lips. He tasted musky, and I slobbed his knob until I had to come up for air. His big mushroom cap head filled my mouth, cutting off my throat and causing drool to run out of the corners of my mouth. I pulled on his big ball sack while I ran up and down over his long shaft with my lips and tongue. The protruding veins on his cock felt like the bumps on a French tickler, and I almost swooned imagining what it was going to feel like to be fucked by this magnificent piece of meat.

Holding his hot cock up to his hairy belly, I licked and sucked my way to his big swinging nut sack. I hoovered it inside my mouth, getting a large dose of his bristly black hair for my effort. Rolling his balls around with my tongue, I simultaneously stroked the sensitive vein on the underside of his shaft with my thumb.

"That's it," he said forcibly as he pulled his ball sack out of my shocked mouth. "I can get a blow job anywhere. It's your ass that I want." I started to stand, and he commanded, "Stay there until I tell you to move."

Electric currents shot through me, tingling my every nerve. This was the kind of man that I needed, one that knew how to command me. I sat back on my heels and waited, wincing from the soreness of my ass cheeks from his earlier spanking.

Chase approached over me and said, "Open your mouth, young one."

I did, and he spit a giant loogie into my mouth.

"Swallow."

I did.

"I'm going to fill you up with all of me," he whispered, a hint of a threat in his tone.

I didn't think I was in danger, except from getting my asshole rubbed raw, so the threat didn't do anything except turn me on even further.

"Stand."

I followed his command, swallowing hard.

"Move over in front of the bed." He waited while I complied. "Put your palms flat on the mattress." I watched from this bent-over position as he walked to one of the nightstands and pulled out a tube of lube. Chase smirked at me as he walked back behind me. The familiar sound of a cock being lubed came next.

I prepared myself for what was to come next. The lube was thick and slightly oily as he poured it onto the top of my ass crack. He rubbed it into my ass crack, up and down my furrow, until he stopped on my puckered hole.

"I've seen a lot of assholes in my day and yours is very small. I'm not sure you'll be able to take me."

I turned around and smirked back at him. "How about we

give it a shot, Sir, or do you want to just stand around and talk about it some more?"

"Oh, I'm going to fuck you up," he growled, pushing two thick fingers against my rosebud. My anal ring spread apart, sending waves of pleasure and pain throughout my body. His fingers probed and swirled inside me, making me buck and gyrate wildly above that bed. My ass felt like it was radiating heat from the spanking, and now every little scrape or touch sent new fingers of hot flame running up my spine.

"We're about to find out whether you can take me or not." Chase pulled his thick fingers out of my ass and placed his velvety cock head against me. The heat from his skin was like hot wax from a candle, burning me while illuminating my desire for him at the same time.

There was a pause as the world stopped turning on its axis and I waited for a man that I was enamored with to push his gigantic cock inside me. My breathing was rapid, but I could hear that his was very controlled. Waiting was torture, but I knew that Christmas was seconds away.

And when it came, it was like the best day Santa ever even thought about. With a deep grunt, Chase pushed his hips forward, driving his goalpost straight into me. My back arched and my head jerked back as he filled me up. Never had my asshole had been stretched so far and so completely.

Chase reached around my waist with his huge muscled arm and held me in place as he pushed the rest of himself into me. The big cockhead punched my prostate, sending another series of pleasurable feelings up my spine. Once Chase was completely buried inside me, I could feel his bush tickling my ass cheeks and the root of his cock spreading me even further apart.

"Fuck me!" Chase roared, pressing his thick, hairy legs against mine. "There's not many people who can take that monster all the way to the root!"

I realized I was holding my breath and let it go in one long exhalation. Chase's cock fit inside my hole like I had been made for it. Once he was inside me, there was nothing else that I needed in the world. I had never felt anything like it, and I knew that I needed him inside me every day from now on.

Chase held me in place and began to fucking tear me up. He knew just what he was doing, fucking me with equal parts speed and finesse. Pulling his cock out until just the gorgeous head remained, he quickly slammed it back home, slamming his body into mine with the thrust.

"Fucking fine piece of tail," Chase said, his voice heady with need and desire.

"Fucking me up, sir." The top of my head was now on the mattress, riding Chase's thrusts into me, acting like a shock absorber. I started to deploy my favorite sexual trick on him, squeezing his cock with my ass muscles as he pulled his big shaft out of me.

I heard him grunt in surprise the first time I squeezed him and almost stop in mid-stroke the second time. He must have decided that he liked it, because he didn't hesitate anymore and went back to driving me onto that mattress.

Chase continued to bury himself into me, going faster and harder with every thrust. Soon he drove inside me, held in place, and yelled in delight as he sprayed hot cum bursts inside my ass.

"Oh, Goddamn!" Chase said, starting to thrust into me again. He was pushing against the sensitivity from his climax. He wrapped his other giant arm around me and pushed me flat onto the bed. He undulated his hips, driving that magnificent cock farther into me again and again.

"Fuck, I gotta get another piece of that," he said, breathing heavily on my back.

"I guess it fit inside then, sir?" I asked, all smart-assed

innocence.

"That fucking smart mouth, again." He smacked my ass hard with a flat hand that left my cheek stinging and reminded me about the spanking he had given me earlier. "Yes, it fit like a glove."

"Like a fucking glove," I echoed.

Chase pulled back, popping his cock out of my hole, and ordered, "Flip over onto your back."

All I knew was that I was grinning like a fool when I flipped over.

"What's so funny, young one?"

"I just wanted to watch you as you work me over, sir, and I'm happy that you are going to let me." From this angle, I could see almost all of him as he worked his magic.

His dark hair was soaked with sweat and was mussed up over his forehead. His unshaven face had formed into a dark beard around his chin that thinned out up to his ears and under his nose. Noticing his nose for the first time, I loved how small and straight it was and the perfect distance above his smirking pale pink lips. His light gray eyes were sheltered under that heavy brow that was defined by his black, thick eyebrows.

Chase held my legs up and back against my chest, signaling me to hold them down for him. He spread my legs apart while I held them, then inspected my little puckered hole. He seemed to enjoy touching and looking at it, so I pushed my ass closer to his face.

He smiled down at me and then spit a big loogie onto my rosebud. I watched, fascinated as he rubbed his spit into my skin and then pushed it inside me. He used two fingers to hold my anal ring open and then spit directly inside me this time. He grinned a huge fucking smile and winked at me.

I was mesmerized as he fed his already-hard cock back into my sore little asshole again. I had my ankles up on his broad shoulders when he fully penetrated me, ripping me in two as he pounded into me.

"Fuck me! How are you so fucking tight, again? I just tore you up and you are as tight as before I touched you."

"Your giant cock will loosen me up, sir."

He took the hint and began to saw me in half as he fucked that giant prick into me. His perfectly muscled thick chest was covered at the top in his dark, course hair, and I pinched his beautiful nipples that hung onto the crease of his perfect pecs. Chase moaned as he rammed and bucked into me.

There was nothing in the world for a marked man that compared to being under a NOMAR who knew how to fuck. For me, this was one step above that because not only was I under a NOMAR who knew how to fuck, but that NOMAR was someone who I had lusted after for over a year, he was physically my perfect man, and he was the best fuck of my life. I had never experienced anything like it before.

Chase came hard and fast, pulling his big cock out of my sore hole, holding it around the shaft in his meaty hand, and pumping its sweet payload right onto my chest and stomach.

"Holy fuck!" he yelled, sluicing his sloppy cock back into my winking hole and driving it home several times.

"Sir, that was . . . the most . . . fantastic fuck . . . of my life." I was winded and made a mental note to myself that I was going to need to get more fit. I would need to work out harder if this was going to be how my life was going to go in The Service.

"You were incredible," Chase said with his mouth barely moving. "The only person I ever fucked who was tighter than you was a virgin, a NOMAR as a matter of fact, and the second time I fucked him was not as good as the second time I fucked you."

"High praise, sir," I said with a smirk.

He dipped a big calloused forefinger into his pool of cum

on my stomach and raised it to my lips. I greedily licked the cum off of his digit and then sucked his finger into my hot mouth while his gray eyes watched my every move.

"I don't usually praise at all, so you're lucky," he told me, returning my smirk.

CHAPTER SIX

Chase fucked me two more times that night before he let me fall asleep. His stamina was amazing, and I was a ragdoll by the time he was finished. I might have fallen asleep while he fucked me from the side, spooning me with his big body, making me feel safe.

The next thing that I became aware of was a familiar voice calling my name.

"Brand, Brand."

I sat partially up and rubbed my eyes. My ass immediately reminded me what had happened last night and how many times. I blinked to adjust my vision and saw my Master at the foot of the bed.

"Master?" I could see Chase McIntyre lying on his stomach beside me. He was naked and on top of the covers.

"Brand, could you do me a favor and put your finger on McIntyre's asshole?"

"Master?" I repeated.

"I need him awake, and it's his alarm," Marshall said by way of explanation.

I hesitated, but followed through with his orders. Master was grinning like a fool, and when I put my finger against Chase's puckered hole, I saw him wince in anticipation.

Chase McIntyre roared like a wounded lion and literally jumped off of the bed. He jerked his head towards me and then saw Marshall at the foot of the bed.

"Taylor, you fucking asshole!" Chase roared.

"Careful, McIntyre, I'm the one who just let you break in

40

one of my Servants all night long."

Some of the fight left Chase and he shrugged. "Well, you got me there. It was so fucking worth it, too."

"So, Brand treated you well?" Master turned to me.

"Amazing." Chase also turned towards me and I got that uncomfortable sensation one gets when everyone is focused on you.

"Amazing?" Master asked, smirking himself.

I was also surprised by the word, but knew better than to talk until I was asked a specific question.

"Yes, amazing." Chase walked over and hugged my Master, even though he was completely naked. "And thanks, man, for him."

"Your welcome, but now that I hear that he is amazing, I am regretting my decision a little bit."

"What's up now? Do you want him back?"

Marshall grabbed his best friend around the shoulders and turned both of their bodies towards me. "I was going to wake you up to go work out, but now that I see how happy you are with Brand, I'm wondering if we should just get our workout right here."

"Now, that's a great fucking idea," Chase said, starting to laugh. "I was hoping to give him another go this morning, anyway."

"What do you think of that, Brand?"

"I think it's an amazing idea, Master." I held out the key-word, just to be even more annoying.

Master smiled and said, "Did Chase treat you right last night, Brand?"

"It truly was phenomenal, Master."

"Are you sore?"

"Very, but I don't want to miss a chance to have you on top of me, Master."

"Well said!" Marshall said with a smile. "He's sore,

McIntyre. How many times did you poke him?"

Chase looked at me with a quizzical look. I held up four fingers.

"Four? Holy fuck, McIntyre!"

Chase shrugged his shoulders, looking abashed, and said, "He was really, really great!"

Master shed his robe and crawled onto the king-sized bed. "Well, I wanna see what all the fuss is about. Brand, you don't know, but McIntyre doesn't really have too many good things to say about the men he fucks, so I am even more intrigued by his fawning over you."

Chase's grin threatened to outgrow his face as he excitedly jumped onto the bed.

"Master?"

"Yes, Brand?"

"Wouldn't you want to wait until I'm . . ."

"Until you are less sore?"

"No, until I'm clean, Master." I looked down in shame. It was one of our mandates as a Servant to always be clean and ready to be fucked for our Masters. I chided myself for falling down on the job and sleeping instead of cleaning myself.

"I'll give you a couple of minutes to prepare yourself, but I really don't mind getting sloppy seconds after my buddy, McIntyre, here."

"Thank you, Master."

Within minutes, I was almost presentable and headed back out to the bed. Master and Chase were both propped up against the headboard, talking. I crawled on all fours like a lanky cat towards their bait between their legs.

I went to Master's crotch first, sucking his semi-hard cock into my mouth. He responded right away, growing hard and radiating heat in full force. I could taste that he had not bothered cleaning himself like I had.

Pulling his cock out of my mouth and using my thumb to

stroke it, I said, "Master had a fun night last night as well, I taste."

"Get your fucking mouth back on there," Master commanded, starting to laugh at me and pushing my head back into his crotch.

I continued to blow him while he told Chase about his night.

"Brand's right, I did have a great time last night."

"You spent it with Jeremy and . . ."

"Braden." I moved over to Chase's lap and sucked his big monster. He was already hard, and I thought it had to be from his need to pee, but he didn't seem bothered by it in the least. I tasted a very similar mélange of tastes on his cock.

"They were pretty good?"

"Braden's mouth is unbelievable and Jeremy is a little fucking machine," Master said, laughing. "You want to try them out?"

"I'm sure I will eventually, but I'm kinda going to stick with Brand here, if it pleases you."

That was like music to my ears, and I looked up to see him smiling down at me. I came off of his cock and moved back over to Master's big dick, who was staring at his friend.

"Good God, Chase!"

"What?" he asked, defensively.

"I've never heard you not excited to fuck the next piece of tail."

"Why give up something great for the unknown?" he reasoned, with a shrug of his shoulders.

Master reached down, cupped my chin in the open space between his raised thumb and his straight forefinger and locked eyes with me. "What have you done with my ass-hound of a best friend, Brand?"

I let his long cock pop out of my mouth, "Nothing that I won't do to you also, Master."

"Oh, his smart mouth makes me so fucking hot," Master snorted. He jacked his cock and moved towards me.

"Lube him up, young one," Chase McIntyre commanded me.

"I think you like bossing him around when he uses that smart mouth," Marshall said to Chase as I worked his cock over with the lube. I loved the feel of Master's velvety soft cock and was, again, impressed by his length.

"That I do! Now, how do you want him, Master Marshall?" Chase asked jokingly.

"Let's roast him, huh, Chase?" Master asked quickly, suddenly pleased with himself.

"Awesome," Chase said, crawling up to the head of the bed. I rose onto all fours and Master's cockhead was soon knocking on my back door. My head was buried in Chase's crotch and my nose full of his masculine scent when Master pushed his hips forward and slowly sank into me.

"God damn, that's tight!" he exclaimed. He buried himself to the balls in me, pulling my ass back onto his cock by holding my hips and pulling them back. "I thought you railed him out four times, McIntyre?"

"I did," Chase said with awe in his voice. "Suck my fat cock, Servant," he teased me.

I nestled my face into Chase's musky crotch, breathing in deeply before sucking his big member into my hungry hole. Master began to fucking rip me a new asshole by pounding into me with some force. I was worried about hurting Chase with my teeth as Master drove me onto his post farther and farther.

Apparently, these best friends had shared more than just *a love for the game of football*. They both knew how to fuck! I used my ass muscles to squeeze Master's cock while it pistoned out of me, hearing him grunt his satisfaction with me each time. Master put on quite a display at some points, causing me to have to come off of Chase's member and hang my head to try to catch my breath.

"You are riding him now, Taylor!" Chase would yell when this happened. It was obvious that these two friends were enjoying pleasuring me together.

"Back on his cock, Brand," Marshall said firmly. "Although my first instinct is to reward you for that fantastic ass trick you are working me over with, I think you need us to be firm with you."

"Yes, Master. I always need you to be firm when you are in me." I knew I was being a smart ass, but licked up Chase's cock and then engorged myself on it again, all the while smirking to myself.

Marshall said, "McIntyre, come on my count. Brand, I'll deal with you later."

"Just like a fucking quarterback!" Chase joked.

"Shut your hole and drop a load in my new Servant on three, two, one!" Master was so excited that he went into superfast action, pummeling me with super hard thrusts that left me breathless. He came within a second of his countdown, shooting his hot load straight into my anal channel.

Chase impressed me, as well, by coming almost on cue, just a second behind my Master. His cum spurted out of his piss-hole with great force, stinging the back of my throat. I swallowed quickly, because cum kept flowing out of him. After a few swallows, I was able to hold some of his sweet cream in my mouth and actually savor it.

Chase's nut juice was salty and smooth on my tongue. It was strong, just like him, and I suddenly couldn't get enough of it. I milked his cock with my hand and mouth to try to get it to produce more. He readily complied, keeping my mouth filled up with it.

"Fuuuuuccccckkkk!" they both groaned, bucking and gyrating behind and in front of me.

Chase looked down at me and said, "Show me, young one."

I let his softening cock fall out of my mouth and opened my mouth, showing Chase the last of his wad.

"Very good." Chase spit a hocker into my open mouth and said, "Marshall, bring your cock up here and let Brand combine our loads in his mouth."

Marshall pulled out of me and climbed up to my face. I worked over his long log, smearing Chase's cum onto Master's cock before sucking it clean again.

"Jesus," Master whispered.

"Fucking yes!" Chase exhaled. "And you wonder why I want to keep fucking around with Brand?"

"You're not the only one . . ."

CHAPTER SEVEN

A fter taking a really long hot shower, I finally felt like I was somewhat normal again, although I would not be taking a seat anytime soon. I got dressed in my jock strap, because that was the only stitch of clothing that I currently had available, and made my way down to the kitchen.

Jeremy and Braden were sitting at the marble island, talking. Padding around the corner, I said, "What's up, fellas?"

"Brand, how was it?" Jeremy asked.

"Good. Really good," I said, unable to not grin. "You?"

"Master is a good fuck," Braden said with a smile of his own.

"I know," I admitted, enjoying the shocked look on their faces.

"He left us to work out early this morning," Jeremy added.

"I must have been the work out."

Jeremy pushed a chair out for me, but I just shook my head.

"Weren't you still with Chase McIntyre?" Braden asked.

"Yes, but that didn't stop Master from sampling his purchase this morning. They spit-roasted me."

Jeremy was still shocked that I wouldn't sit down. "How many times?"

I looked at him coyly and asked, "How many times what?"

He cocked his head to the side at my game play and said, "Did you get fucked?"

"This morning, only once."

The look he gave me was withering.

"I don't know about him, but each one of Master's friends

47

fucked me and blew in my mouth last night." We all turned to see Alex walk up to the island with a big-ass grin on his face.

"No way," Braden whispered.

"Yeah, they kept me busy. See if you can top that, Brand," he challenged.

"Chase fucked me four times last night," I finally told them.

"Jesus. I was afraid with four Servants and only one Master that we weren't going to have enough cock to go around," Jeremy admitted.

We all laughed, telling him that he had nothing to worry about. We scrounged around for something to eat, finally finding a box of cereal and digging in. The four of us seemed to mix pretty well, and the conversation flowed easily. Alex also stood at the island with me, unwilling to sit through the pain.

We were still in this position, having loaded the dishwasher and cleaned up, when Master and Chase walked into the house. They were both sweaty and smelly from the gym, but were still totally hot.

"Well, well. Here are my boys!" Master said excitedly, as he looked at us all together.

"Master," I said in acknowledgement. Two of the boys fell down into The Service Squat.

"You may stand or sit. You boys did a very good job last night. I have talked to all of my crew and they had a great time."

The four of us were all smiles.

"Let's go upstairs." Master and Chase turned and headed up the stairs. I looked over at the others and then scurried after them.

Master kept climbing the stairs and without turning around, said, "I'm so happy with you guys that we are going to do a little shopping for you today."

Awesome! I didn't relish spending the next year in this jock strap.

Master stopped at the first door on the floor and said, "Braden and Alex will sleep in here." This was news to us. I hadn't even given any thought to where I would sleep.

We passed Master's room, and across the hall from the bedroom that Chase used, we stopped again. "Jeremy and Brand will use this room."

I smiled at Master and felt Chase's eyes burning for me.

"I'm going to shower now and would like Alex to join me." Alex's face lit up immediately. Master turned to his best friend and asked, "And who would you like to shower with, Chase?"

"I would like Brand." He was staring at me, but then turned to his friend and added, "If that is okay with you, Marshall."

"Of course. Alex, let's go." Master seemed less surprised this time, but I saw something on his face that I wasn't able to identify. I would have to process that later, when I didn't have the visions of a naked, wet Chase McIntyre in front of me.

Chase motioned with his head to his room, and I felt bad for Jeremy and Braden being left behind. I was grateful to have Chase want me and told myself to reward him amply for it. I half-smiled to the boys I was leaving behind and followed one of the hottest men I had ever seen into his bedroom.

Once the door was shut, he commanded, "Strip." His voice was husky with need.

"Yes, sir," I said slowly as I hooked a thumb into the elastic strap going around my waist and pushed it sideways. My jock was now off-center and I turned ever so slightly to give him a side view of my ass, as well.

His gaze never left my body and he ran his big pink tongue

over his lips. "Now, you are just asking for it."

"Seems like I am always asking for it, sir," I said with a coy smile.

"And I am always giving it to you, aren't I?"

"Yes, sir. You are one of the few people I have met in my life who can wear me out." I hooked the other thumb into the other side of my jock strap and pushed it down.

"But?" he asked, correctly reading between my words.

"I don't want you to get tired of me, sir." As I said this, I bent over in front of him to pull my jock the rest of the way off. My ass was on full display in front of him, and when he reached out with a big, rough, hairy hand to slightly skim the surface of the skin covering my ass cheek, it sent cold chills running throughout my body.

The cold chills were soon replaced with burning magma running up my spine as he rammed his thumb into my hole, hooked it inside and grabbed hold of a handful of my ass cheek. Chase headed to the shower, pulling me beside him like I was a bowling ball. His thumb was constantly putting pressure on my asshole from the inside, but it wasn't scratching the itch that I was feeling deep inside. However, I knew that he would get to that shortly.

Once in the bathroom, Chase pointed me at the full-wall mirror above the marble-topped basins and removed his hand from my ass. He stripped off his clothes in two quick movements.

"Fuck!" slipped out of my mouth before I could even stop it. I was watching him undress in the mirror and was so completely blown away with his hotness. Chase McIntyre was my perfect man in every way. I still was pinching myself that he was going to fuck me and that it would be the fifth time I found myself in this incredible position.

Chase's light grey eyes locked onto my green ones in the mirror and then he grunted in agreement. His now-familiar smirk slowly started to spread across his face.

"I'm going to fucking rip your tight little hole apart," he promised.

"Again and again, sir."

"You fucking know it!" Chase grabbed the lube, filled the palm of his hand, dipped some fingers into it, and then fed it into my hot honey hole.

"Oh, shit," I moaned.

His fingers were like the propellers on a helicopter, working me around and around inside.

"You like Mac fucking finger-blasting you like that?"

I didn't know he had a nickname, but it suited him somehow. "Yes, sir."

"Good!" He immediately vexed me by pulling his thick digits out of me, causing my asshole to snap shut. His eyes never left mine in the mirror. He slicked his thick cock and said, "Don't worry, little one, I'm going to give you what you need in just a minute."

"Yes, sir." I tried not to sound impatient, but it was hard, just like I was. And so was this gorgeous man who was all mine, at least for the next hour or so. I drank him in as he walked to the toilet and sat down on the lid. His leg muscles rippled as he walked, making a beautiful line that accentuated his furry ass.

By the time Chase had removed his tennis shoes and athletic socks, revealing his beautiful big feet, I was absolutely salivating for him. He watched me watching him, which caused my raging hard-on to ache as it throbbed against the cold marble of the countertop.

Chase slowly rose from the toilet and padded to me. He stood directly behind me so that I couldn't see him in the mirror. Suddenly there was a slap on the countertop beside my hip. I looked down to see Chase's hunky foot resting against me.

"Lick it," he commanded.

He didn't have to order me twice. I bent sideways and ran my tongue over the tops of his toes and the hairy skin over the top of his foot. I didn't even look up to see if I had pleased him, because I knew I had and because I was loving the way his sweaty, manly foot was tasting on my tongue.

"Suck my toes," he commanded next.

My licks continued, but on the inside of my mouth. I had sucked Chase's big toe and his second toe into my mouth. Savoring the salty taste of his toes, I was completely distracted, and he took advantage. With one strong movement he pushed me forward over the countertop, and with a thrust of his thighs and hips, Chase McIntyre entered my puckered hole, stretching my anal ring wide.

I moaned around his thick toes, my body tensing as Chase slid his complete shaft into my ass. I squeezed him, as if my ass was a hand and I was milking his big tool.

He moaned in appreciation.

It felt like his cock would never hit the bottom of my ass, but finally I felt his bushy crotch tickle my ass cheeks and his nut sack bang into me.

"Oh, fuck! There is no way you can be this fucking tight."

I removed his toes from my mouth and asked, "Am I squeezing you too hard, sir?" I smirked at Chase in the mirror.

He glared at me, a mixture of sheer delight and wanton lust on his face. "Is that all you got, little one?"

*Ah, a challenge . . ."*I give it all to you, sir, every time."

"That I know, little one. And now, I'm going to give it all to you." Chase proceeded to ramrod me with his huge tool, putting on a show of swordsmanship that I had rarely seen before, let alone been a part of. He panted with the effort and I soaked it all in, watching his every movement in the mirror.

"Get that foot back in your mouth."

Rushing to comply, I bent my body towards his foot once

again. I ran my tongue over his delicious skin before sucking his big toe into my greedy mouth. As soon as I started sucking, Chase sighed, arched his back, and fucking jack hammered his cock into my ass.

His aggressiveness was all I needed to send me over the edge of my climax. I came in a hot puddle on the countertop, watching it seep out from every possible fissure created by my stomach and the countertop. My ass muscles immediately snapped even tighter around Chase's poor cock.

"Yes! That's the sweetness I've been waiting for." Chase's voice was one of sheer pleasure and I smiled as I reached for his little toes on the edge of his foot.

Chase's girth was keeping my asshole spread wide open, and the sensation of my stretched hole sliding up and down his hard shaft was more than anything I could have ever dreamed. His cock was so hard that I could have sworn that I could feel every vein on its surface as I rode up and down on it.

His thrusts had increased in pace and we were both sweating profusely by the time he came. Chase roared through his climax, pounding away at my ass, even as his cock spurted hot cum over every inch of my anal canal. I continued to suck on his toes, grunting around them and trying hard not to let my teeth touch his skin as he bucked me back and forth on the counter.

"That's my boy," Chase said, breathily. Once our breathing had returned to normal, he pulled out of me and begun filling the tub with warm water. I stood watching him, mesmerized by his sheer masculinity and drawn to him by our sexual chemistry.

Once the temperature was correct, Chase stepped into the water like a giant black bear entering the stream. His hair glistened with sweat and his muscles rippled under his skin. Was I the luckiest man alive or what?

Chase sat down in the giant garden tub, stretching like a big black cat. He turned to me and said, "Well? Are you going to join me?"

"May I, sir?"

"Of course! You're my boy. I always want you with me."

This was news to me, so I soaked in his praise. *He always wants me with him?* Realizing that I felt the same way about him, I hopped into the tub and took a seat between his legs. I used my foot to caress and rub his chubby cock as it floated on the rising water.

"You want some more of Mac?" he asked with a smirk.

"You're my man. I always want you in me," I smirked.

CHAPTER EIGHT

Chase McIntyre planted his seed inside me twice more before we were clean and had exited the bathtub. Just like last night, I was absolutely amazed at his power and stamina. He seemed to like fucking me each time just as much as he had that first time. I didn't know if this was normal or not, but I was a little concerned that I had only been fucked by my Master once and by his best friend seven times.

Another disturbing fact was that I thought I was falling for Chase. He was perfect! He was my football fantasy masturbation dream come true, and much to my surprise, he was everything I could ever ask for him to be. It really worried me that I was developing this bond so quickly and that it was not with my Master.

As far as I was concerned, I was going to have to worry about this later, because my ass was still smarting from Chase's pounding, and it was really hard to stay focused on anything but his giant tool. Later that afternoon, I tried to pull it together for a meeting that Master wanted to have with us.

All of the Servants gathered in the kitchen to wait for Master to speak with us. Chase nodded at me as he left for his house.

"He's enraptured with you," Braden whispered.

"No, he just likes my tight ass," I replied, blushing.

"Well, whatever it is, he's all about you."

"How many times did he fuck you while you were showering?" Jeremy asked.

"Three."

"Son of a bitch! I wish I was getting that much cock," Jeremy said, jealousy and disappointment mixed on his face.

Before anyone else could comment, Master walked into the kitchen, looking hot in jeans, sandals, and a tight t-shirt.

"What's up, fellas?"

"Master," I said in a hushed voice. My fellow Servants echoed me.

"I have some goodies for you guys," he said excitedly as he went into the hallway and came back with a big brown shipping box. He put it down on the island and opened it up. Master pulled out a lot of clothing in plastic bags. "These are wind pants, t-shirts, mesh shorts from the team that should be okay for you guys, at least so we can go shopping today."

The four of us tore into the clothing. The sizes were all over the place, but we swapped around until we were all covered. By the time we were done, the four of us looked like we were the cheer squad for the New York Colossals, but we were covered. All four of us had pairs of rubber sandals to match the ones Master was wearing.

Master stepped back and regarded us. "Looks good. Shall we go?"

It was our first field trip with Master, and we were all excited. I wasn't used to not being told where we were going, but that just added to the excitement. We all went into a garage, and I was amazed at Master's collection of cars. There were also motorcycles and quads tucked in front of the four automobiles. I had never seen a garage so big, and I was floored by Master's nonchalance about it. I told myself that obviously if he could afford four Servants, then he could afford all kinds of toys.

Master held the back door of a huge white Tahoe open for us. Alex, Braden, and I jumped in the back, and Jeremy rode up front with Master. Marshall hit a button which raised one of the garage doors and pulled out into the brilliant autumn sunshine. He drove us down a large driveway which had a security station at the bottom.

I'm not sure why I was surprised by the fact that Master was so well protected, because, after all, he was a superstar athlete and a celebrity. Master spoke to the guard on duty and the gate opened. We sat waiting. What for, I wasn't sure.

Master reached for the radio and said, "What kind of music do you guys like?"

I looked over at Alex, who shrugged.

Jeremy answered, "Country, Master."

"You guys?" Master asked, looking in the rearview mirror.

"Classical, Master," Alex said.

"Top forty, Master," Braden said, surprising me, yet again.

"Top forty, Master," I echoed.

I watched, fascinated as Master programmed the radio with a few different satellite stations and then hit play. *Royals* by Lorde boomed through the speakers. Before the song was over, a black Escalade pulled out in front of us and Master put the car into gear. The song switched to *Four Seasons* by Vivaldi, and I reasoned that he had programmed songs from each of our genres into the radio. He was very accommodating for a Master.

Now I knew why we were waiting, apparently for our escort of security guards. Being with a celebrity was going to be a whole new experience for me. Every pothole and bump in the road reminded me of my morning with Chase McIntyre, and I found myself daydreaming about him and wondering what he was doing.

We soon pulled into the parking lot of a Marshall's and stopped. Master sat in the car, whistling to a new Thomas Rhett country song. I watched out of the window as the team of security guards in the car ahead us headed into the store. Some of them stayed behind, standing by our car. A call was finally made and we were waved out of the car.

The five of us headed into the store and Master told us, "You guys each get a shopping cart to fill up. Don't come back with it empty. I will have a tailor come to the house to measure you for suits, so just get the basics that you need here."

We all looked at him with awe.

He continued, "Don't forget anything. I only want to have to do this once."

It was an effective strategy, because none of us wanted to displease him.

"Go," was his simple command when we reached the shopping carts.

I didn't know how much time he was giving us, so I decided to go as quickly as I could. I felt like we were on one of those game shows where you had to shop till you dropped.

Heading for the shirts, I realized that I was in pretty good shape, because I was taller and bigger than the other Servants. I would not be competing with them for the same sizes. My cart was soon full of t-shirts, dress shirts, shorts, jeans, underwear, belts, swimsuits, socks, and work-out gear. The one thing I couldn't find was shoes. I didn't like anything in my size, and I wondered whether I should just get them anyway.

I was still contemplating my decision when I saw Master at the end of my aisle in a conversation with another customer who seemed to be a fan. I watched, fascinated, as Marshall Taylor tried to move away and the fan followed. The security guards were there, but they must have felt there was no danger, so they were not interfering. Master was trying not to be rude, but couldn't shake the fan.

Deciding on the fly what to do, I headed towards them down the aisle. As I approached, I raised my voice and said, "Mr. Taylor, I need to see you on an urgent private matter."

Master, who had his back towards me, turned around and looked at me with a stunned look on his face. Then his beautiful smile crept across his face.

"Of course." He turned back to the fan and said, "It was nice meeting you, but I need to handle this."

The fan nodded his head gravely and said his farewells. Master turned and quickly covered the distance to me, pulling me with him down the aisle.

"Thanks for that, Brand. I couldn't get away from him."

"No problem, Master." We walked down to my cart and he pretended to inspect the contents.

"Did you find everything?"

I swallowed hard, deciding to tell him my dilemma. "I don't like any of their shoes, Master." I knew I could be punished for it, but I didn't think he would.

"No?" Marshall looked at me with his kind blue eyes.

I hung my head and said, "I'll get some anyway, Master."

"No. You're a Taylor now. We don't settle. We're not pretentious, but we get what we want."

I looked up at him, smiling.

"We'll just have to go to a shoe store," he said, grinning back at me.

"Thank you, Master."

"No problem," he said, repeating my words from earlier. We walked back to the check-out, pushing my cart followed by Master's bodyguards. Jeremy and Alex were waiting there with their carts.

Master turned to look back, didn't see Braden anywhere, and said, "Well, let's go ahead and get started checking-out, and hopefully he will join us before we finish."

Jeremy pushed his cart into the line and the cashier started to ring him up. Jeremy's purchases totaled over two hundred dollars. Alex was next and his spending was almost two hundred dollars. I pushed my cart into the line and saw Braden approach us, his cart so loaded down with clothes that it was mounded over the top like a turtle's shell.

I shook my head in the universal symbol of disapproval,

noticing out of the corner of my eye that Master was laughing at me.

"Jesus, Braden," Jeremy blurted out.

My purchases came in behind Jeremy's and before Alex's, and I made sure to thank Master for them. We all watched with fascination as Braden unloaded his sleigh. His purchases totaled more than four hundred dollars. We all watched Master's face to see his reaction, but he was circumspect with his emotions. He did nothing but smile as the cash register showed the final tally.

Master helped us to the car with our bags, saying, "Now to the shoe store." We had to fight through a mass of fans that had gathered in front of the store waiting to see Master.

I got two pair of tennis shoes, two pair of dress shoes, and a pair of bedroom slippers. The other guys got a few pairs of shoes, and we soon were on our way home, after going through the drive-thru of a Wendy's for lunch. I wanted a cheeseburger, but got peer-pressured into getting a salad with chicken on it.

As soon as we were home, Master helped carry our bags into the house. I was excited to unpack my clothes into the bedroom that Jeremy and I shared, but Master wanted to talk to us first.

"You guys did really well today," Master beamed.

"Is there any way we can thank you, Master?" I asked, raising an eyebrow to just make my point ridiculously obvious.

"I think you all can thank me in your own special way." He smiled at all of us. "We're going to play a little round of speed fucking!"

I looked at the other Servants, and they looked just as clueless as I was.

"Each of you will have ten minutes alone with me and an additional five minutes in tandem with the next Servant. I suggest that you use the time wisely." Master smirked at us, reminding me of his best friend.

I couldn't help but smile at him. I was loving the idea of this game, and the fact that Master was so excited about it, made it that much better.

"Brand, you're first." Master turned on his heel and headed upstairs. I smiled at the fellas before rushing after him. I stripped my clothes off as I hurried up the stairs. By the time I made it to his bedroom, I was completely naked.

Master got to the bed and turned around, bursting into laughter.

"I didn't want to waste any time, Master," I said, embarrassed.

"Excellent! I'm glad you didn't." He shucked off his clothes, and I was delighted to see that he was already hard.

I knelt before my Master and sucked his long cock into my mouth. The head of his cock poked the back of my throat, causing me not to be able to suck it all the way in. I worked him over with my hand while I worked my magic with my tongue.

Master was hard as a rock in a minute, so I stood and asked, "How would you like me, Master?"

"On your back."

I lay back onto the bed, noticing that there was already a bottle of lube on the bed, plus Master's cell phone, which was in stopwatch mode. I shifted back onto the middle of the bed and lubed my hole. Master came up between my legs, and I used the rest of the lube on his long hot cock. I rubbed it between my two palms, getting it as slick as I could. The pressure of the short time I was allowed was constantly in the back of my mind. Lifting my feet, I placed them on his chest and awaited his assault on my ass.

Master placed his big cockhead on my puckered hole and held it there, throbbing against me. "I've wanted to do this ever since you saved me from that fan in the store."

"Thanks for everything you have done for us, Master."

"You are welcome, and I'm going to thank you right now." With those words, he winked at me and shoved his massive tool through my anal ring and inside of me. I groaned and arched my back, forcing my ass closer to Marshall's crotch, therefore impaling myself on his long cock even further.

"Jesus! If I know my friend McIntyre, he's been tearing your little asshole up for the past few days. How then are you so tight?"

"It's just for you, Master."

"I doubt that, but it is exceptional. You showered with Mac this morning?"

"Yes, sir."

"And how many times did he fuck you?"

It was not something I wanted to brag about to my Master, but I was compelled to answer him. "Three times, Master." Normally, I would have looked down, but in this position, there was nowhere to look to avoid his eyes.

"Well, then, I'd better get to it. I'm behind, literally." Master and I laughed as he started to thrust back and forth into my ass.

Realizing that I was short on time, I squeezed his cock hard with my ass muscles, milking him as he fucked me. I held onto his biceps as I rocked back and forth under him. He sheathed his sword and then pulled it out again and again.

"Fuck me!" he finally moaned, burying himself deeply inside and falling over his climax. Master lifted my legs, one ankle in each of his big hands, and separated them so he could pound his big stick into me several more times.

Suddenly, beside me on the bed, Master's phone alarm beeped.

"Alex!" he yelled. Master smacked me on the ass as he pulled his cummy cock out of me. "Ten minutes . . . impressive, Brand."

"Thanks, Master."

Alex burst into the room, stripping his clothes off as quickly as he could. He had a panicked look on his face.

"Come on, Alex. I'll help you get him hard again." I was nothing if not a team player. I was going to clean up his sloppy cock, but Alex was on it before I could even say anything.

Master lay back on the comforter, and I sucked his nipple into my mouth while tweaking the other one between my fingers. Alex was sucking him like a vacuum cleaner, playing with his balls at the same time. Coming off of his nipples, I moved down to his skinny little feet. Massaging them with my thumbs and fingers before licking the bottoms of each, I took my time and made sure I had his attention. I watched Master's face as I performed and I saw his eyes widen as he realized what was going to happen.

Just when it was getting good, his alarm rang and I put up my hands like a contestant on Top Chef just finishing his dish.

"Thanks, Brand," Master said with a smile.

"Thank you again, Master."

Alex raised his eyebrows while Master's long cock was completely down his throat, signaling me his pleasure at my help. I walked out of the bedroom, gathering my shoes and clothes along the way. Closing the door quietly behind me, I saw Jeremy and Braden pacing outside the door.

"You fellas look nervous as hell," I said, starting to laugh.

"Ten minutes is no time at all," Braden fretted.

"Were you able to *thank him*?" Jeremy asked.

"Yeah." I was very proud of this fact, and also aware that it would be harder and harder for the guys after me to get him to climax.

"With the extra five minutes and Alex helping?" Braden asked.

"No, before he came in, actually."

"No way!" Braden exclaimed, disbelief on every part of his face.

"You can do it, too," I told them as I started to blush. "I helped Alex get Master ready to go again with my last five minutes. I suggest you guys do the same for each other, if you're going to properly thank him for today."

CHAPTER NINE

Jeremy and I had finished up Master with a furious five minutes that allowed Jeremy to ride Marshall's cock as he came for the fourth time in an hour. Master was so happy with the four of us that he had a smile on his face as he fell asleep. Jeremy and I snuck out of his bedroom and into the hallway.

Braden and Alex were waiting on us, and I held my finger up to my lips so they would whisper.

"He's asleep," Jeremy said.

"I'm going to go shower," I stated matter-of-factly.

"Right behind you," Jeremy added. Once inside our bedroom, I stripped out of my clothes and headed to the bathroom. I turned on the water and tested it.

"Mind if I join you?" Jeremy asked from the doorway. He was completely naked and had that short, muscular body that really turned me on. I imagined me holding onto that thick neck as I fucked him hard.

Snapping myself out of that fantasy, I said, "Sure!" I could hear my voice and knew that it wasn't normal.

The water was warm enough, so I stepped inside and held the glass shower door for Jeremy. He gingerly stepped inside and I moved back to make room for him. Jeremy turned and his ass brushed my legs. I knew what he was doing, but was unwilling to resist.

"On your knees," I commanded.

I could see his eyes widen in the shaving mirror and knew that this was what he needed.

He immediately turned and lowered himself to the shower

floor. I placed my palm flat on his shaggy head and pushed back. His head pivoted up and I held his eyes with mine.

"Suck that big cock, boy." I changed my voice, talking an octave deeper and with absolute confidence. The familiar twinge in my crotch told me that I was starting to get excited.

Jeremy quickly licked his lips as I pushed his head into my crotch. He held my big dick by the base as he sucked it inside his hungry mouth. I loved the sensation of being blown and Jeremy did not disappoint. I had both of my hands on his head, guiding his movements. I stayed in control, holding his head still and face-fucking him by thrusting my hips forward repeatedly.

His spit ran down the sides of his mouth as he soaked the shaft of my cock. He had my joint nicely lubed and I knew, with a load of Master's inside him already, that would be all he would need. I pulled my cock out of his mouth and slapped him across the face with it. He tried to capture it back into his mouth, but I was ready to sample his sweet ass.

"Stand!" I commanded. Jeremy looked really cute as the shower water streamed over him, soaking his hair and making his skin glisten.

"Put your arms around my neck." I saw the realization on his face when he discovered what I was planning. He reached up and locked his fingers behind my neck.

I picked him up by his ass cheeks, and he spread his legs, eventually wrapping them around my waist.

"You ready, boy?" I asked, my voice deep and husky with need.

"Yes, sir," he responded, his eyes never leaving mine.

I let go of him with one hand and used the other to spread his ass cheeks apart. My free hand was on my wet cock, guiding it to his hole. For such a small guy, he certainly had a big asshole. Placing my cockhead against his puckered skin, I checked to see if he was ready.

"I'm going to fucking tear you up, little one!" I used one of Chase McIntyre's favorite lines because I knew what it did to me when he said it. The look in Jeremy's eyes told me that my words were hitting home for him as well.

"Yes, sir. Thank you, sir."

"Don't give me that rote bullshit," I seethed. His eyes widened in shock.

"Sorry, sir."

"Fucking right," I said as I pushed my hips forward and buried my cock inside him. My cock was just a little shorter than Master's, but with more girth. Jeremy's anal ring spread wide around the shaft of my cock as I sank into him up to my nuts.

"Oh, fuck," Jeremy sighed.

"Shut your fucking hole!" I commanded.

Jeremy slowly shut his gaping mouth and then, ever so slowly, his lips curled into a smirk.

I fucking tore that smirk off of his face. I fucked his hole so fast and hard that Jeremy bit his lower lip to keep from making a sound. He bounced on my big joystick, my ball sack slapping the top of his ass with every stroke. Jeremy held his head back and grunted with each of my thrusts.

Even though I was enjoying this fucking, I secretly hoped that my hole was a lot tighter than Jeremy's. His ass felt good on my cock, but he wasn't milking me the way that I tried to work Chase and Marshall. I didn't know whether that made me special or made Jeremy not special. Either way, I enjoyed jarring Jeremy's teeth with this fuck.

"Tell me how much you want me to keep fucking you."

"Don't stop, sir," Jeremy begged.

I reached down and grabbed his cock. It was hard, and I squeezed it while I put his back against the tiled wall. My body weight held Jeremy on the wall while I fucked into him with some speed and power.

"I need it. I need it hard, sir."

"You're a real cock whore, aren't you?" I was out of breath, but tried my best not to show it.

"Yes, sir. Fucking give it to me, sir."

"Pump your cock for me."

Jeremy took over from me working his tool. I felt my climax building, and it didn't take long before it arrived. Jamming my cock as far into him as I could, I busted my nut and coated his anal chamber with hot sperm. Jeremy was right behind me, his cock shooting hot strands of cum between our chests.

"Oh my fucking God," Jeremy moaned as I began to nail his asshole again, milking the last bit of cum out of my fuckstick.

A deep voice suddenly filled the small room. "What the fuck do you think you're doing?" His voice was loud, clear and commanding and I knew who it was instantly.

I stepped back from the wall, Jeremy slid down off of me, and we both turned to see Chase McIntyre staring at us through the glass shower door.

"Well? Brand, don't make me ask again."

My heart felt like it was pounding out of my chest. I thought quickly on my feet and tried to sound convincing. "Master had us do a team challenge and we were just coming off the high, sir."

"Clean up and get out. You have two minutes." Chase turned on his heel and went into our bedroom.

Jeremy and I looked at each other, wide-eyed, not daring to talk. I scrubbed myself clean and hurried out of the shower, barely drying off before joining the man-of-my-dreams, who stood silently, all disappointment and anger. Jeremy quickly joined me.

"Jeremy, get in your cage," he commanded. I hadn't even realized that our cages were in the room, but there they were.

Jeremy looked to the side in shock and then back to Chase, as if to say, *Are you fucking kidding me?*

"Get in the fucking cage!" Chase growled.

His growl turned me on like nothing I had ever heard before. I knew I was in trouble, but no one told my body, which promptly made my cock immediately start to stand at attention. Jeremy dropped to all-fours and scrambled across the room and into his cage.

"Marshall will have to deal with both of you when he wakes up," Chase said as he walked over to the cage, closed the door, and locked the padlock. Then he turned towards me, looked down at my raging hard-on and then said, "Hands behind your back."

What?

I didn't know where he was going, but I followed his commands. I watched, fascinated, while he stepped towards me and pulled zip-ties out of his pocket. He bound my hands behind my back with one quick tug of the zip-tie.

"March."

I started to walk towards my cage, misunderstanding.

"To my room," he growled.

I changed course and headed to the door. Chase sounded mad, but I hoped he wasn't. I couldn't imagine what was going to happen to me, but I also couldn't wait to find out!

Chapter Ten

Chase pushed me head-first onto his bed. My face was turned to the side, but I was unable to see what he was doing. My hearing was also hampered, since one of my ears was pressed into the mattress. I thought I could hear him undressing, but I wasn't sure.

When he climbed onto the bed, I could feel it. He was a big man, and when his weight pressed down the mattress, there was no mistaking it. My balls ached with the anticipation of what was to come.

My hands were painfully bound behind my back. He pushed my thighs up under my stomach, bending my knees. My ass rose gracefully into the air, unprotected from his inevitable assault.

He draped himself over me, his unshaven face scratching my skin. Chase's lips tickled my ear as he whispered, "You've been a very bad boy, Brand."

"Sorry, sir."

"No you're not," he seethed. "You enjoyed fucking that little fireplug! Didn't you?"

"Yes, sir, but not as much as I enjoy getting fucked by you."

"You fucking ripped him apart." His breath on my ear and neck was hot, giving me cold chills and making my cock even harder. I knew not to say anything, since this was a statement.

"I was there for quite a while before I said anything. It was fascinating to watch you dominate him like that. Where did you learn to do that?"

"You, sir." Whether it was the truth or not, I knew this was the only answer I could give. In this case though, it was true. I had picked up many a trick from this man who was domineering over me right now.

"That's what I thought . . . is that what you are, a natural dominant, I mean?

"I don't think so, sir. I am what they call a switch—able to be both dominant and submissive."

"You will be submissive for me?"

"Totally, sir. I want nothing more."

He looked at me with sheer lust in his eyes. "Do you want me to show you some new tricks?"

"Yes, sir."

"That's good. I've got a lot more to show you, baby." Chase lubed his cock and planted it on my puckered hole. I felt completely vulnerable in this position and he knew it.

He pushed his hips forward, drilling into my tiny asshole. I squeezed my eyes shut against the comforter and exhaled, "Oh, fuck me."

"You deserve this." Chase slid completely inside me while colored fireworks went off inside my skull. Once his sword was buried to the hilt inside me, he lay on top of me, completely covering me with his furry muscular body.

His lips were back at my ear as his cock throbbed away inside me like his heartbeat. "It was amazing seeing you dominate Jeremy like that . . . it really turned me on to know that I was going to dominate you right after you dominated him. I'm going to fucking tear you up just like you did him."

I was perfectly okay with that. Chase McIntyre gave me a long, hard fucking that was one for the record books. It felt like my asshole was on fire, being stretched to its limits around Chase's wide cock and being relentlessly pounded by him. He came hard and fast, breathing heavily as he lay on me.

"Holy fuck! I think I'm addicted to your sweet ass. I just

gave you a hard fucking, and all I could think of was that I wanted to do it again."

"I would like that, sir."

His lips were back to my ear. "I need to punish you, but we just keep winding up in this position."

"It's punishment enough knowing that I have disappointed you, sir," I said, half into the comforter.

"On the contrary, I'm quite proud of you. I saw myself in you and I liked it . . . a lot." His voice was heady and he surprised me by rubbing his stubbly cheek against mine.

"Fuck me again, sir. Just so I remember it," I said, my voice full of lust and need. I knew my words would set him off and I was counting on it.

Chase McIntyre didn't disappoint. He got right to work, thrusting his hardening laphog back to the depths of my ass and working himself into a rhythm. I was sweating under the strain of his fuck and his weight pressing down on me. It was a glorious fuck.

Suddenly the door opened and someone walked in. I couldn't see who it was since my head was buried in the mattress, but I recognized the voice.

Master's deep voice echoed in the big bedroom, "Chase, why do you have Brand's hands bound?" I thought it was really big of him to not ask why he was fucking his Servant while he was asleep, but Marshall Taylor was a good friend apparently—a really good friend.

"I came in from running my errands and I found him fucking Jeremy in the shower."

"I'm sorry, Master," I said, as sincerely as I could.

Chase continued, "I locked Jeremy in his cage and came in here to punish Brand . . ." His voice trailed off. My only feeling of connectivity to him was the tether of his cock, which was expanding inside my ass.

"I see that he is getting his just desserts," Marshall said, sarcastically.

"I—"

"I'm just kidding you, Mac!" Master laughed, easily. "I'm just happy that Brand has gotten you to settle down, even if it is at his expense." Master climbed onto the bed, twisting so that I could see his face. He smiled, and I returned his smile the best way that I could.

Master reached over to my face and put his big palm on my cheek, his thumb gliding under my eye. "Brand, is that a tear?"

"I never want to disappoint you or Mr. McIntyre, Master."

He chuckled and said, "Well, if that is the worst thing that you do while you're with me for the next two years, then you will be fine."

"Yes, sir."

Master chuckled and asked, "Did you at least give Jeremy a good railing?"

"You should have seen him, Marshall," McIntyre answered with pride in his voice.

"Perhaps I will soon. This is my fault anyway. I've been so worried about keeping the four of you satisfied that I forgot to ask about your needs."

This was an amazing thing to hear a Master say and it left me completely stunned. Most Masters could have cared less about the needs of their Servants.

I loved this man already. "Can I do anything for you, Master?"

He looked at me fondly for a second and then said, "I would like to have my cock down your throat while you're all trussed up like this and impaled on Mac's huge cock."

"Done," I said.

Master smiled, stripped off his basketball shorts, and shifted so he could straddle my face. Chase grunted in delight behind me and lifted my head off of the mattress by pulling on my bound arms. Marshall slid his crotch under my head while I hovered in the air above him. Chase gently let me down until my cheek was resting on Master's inner thigh and his long trouser-snake was looming large in front of my eyes.

The strain on my arms and shoulders was incredible, and when Chase released my arms, it was like heaven, but I didn't see how I was going to be able to suck him off in this position. But my Master's best friend was way ahead of me. He put one big hand on each of my shoulders and held me up, cantilevered over Master. His big cock firmly planted in my ass held me steady at the other end.

I sucked Master's cockhead into my pie hole and tasted his delicious velvety skin. He must have showered after he woke up from his nap, because he tasted like soap and smelled like mint. I worked as much of him into my mouth as I could, gagging on his length. Chase decided to continue to fuck me while he held me aloft of Master. He rose onto his feet and hunched over my ass, one foot on each side of my hips and began to slide in and out of me at a good even rhythm that allowed me to slide up and down on Master's cock at the same time.

Being between these two big hunks and being spit-roasted on their massive cocks, I was truly in Shangri-la. When I relaxed a little, I was able to take more of Master's long pole into my hungry mouth.

"Oh, shit," Master sighed, throwing his head back. His long legs were spread wide open on either side of me, and I really wished I had my hands to explore him.

"You should feel how tight this shit is, Marsh," Chase grunted, his voice in a rare tone of delight.

"I know he has to be to have captured your attention, McIntyre."

"I've never fucked anything like it before. I just fucked him less than ten minutes ago, never took my dick out of him, and kept him stretched to his limit for a while. Yet he's as tight as a virgin now."

Chase must have been sweating under the strain of hunching, fucking, and holding me up, because his sweat began to drop on my back like giant raindrops. I wanted nothing more than to lick his whole body dry after we were done.

Master started to produce a copious amount of precum, which lubed my mouth and let me swallow more of him. Soon he was punching the back of my throat, so I opened it up for him. At first just the tip of his cock entered my throat and then the stroke after, half of it. The next thing I knew, I was deep-throating him!

"Goddamn!" Marshall spasmed. Chase paused in his assault on my puckered hole. "He's not supposed to be the one that is fantastic at sucking."

Chase chuckled and resumed his work.

"I'm fucking coming," Master warned me, grabbing my head with both hands and pushing his cockhead into my throat. His whole body shook as he shot strands of hot cum directly into my gullet.

"Me, too!" Chase roared, slamming his huge salami into me as far as it would go before erupting in a torrent of hot cum.

I tried to control my breathing and relax, but it was hard — riding those two waves of fulfillment was almost more than I could take. Master finally pulled his cock back from my throat and let me taste his sweet cream while I licked him clean.

"Fuck me," he sighed.

"You want to fuck him now, Marsh?" Chase asked.

"I'd like to, of course, but I can't. I dropped five loads in the past two hours. I'm not a machine like you, Mac, I need to eat!" Master slid off of the bed and started to get dressed.

We all laughed at that as Chase cut the zip cord binding my wrists. They immediately fell to my sides. He pulled out of me and flipped me over. His big rough hands grabbed my wrists and started to massage them. I was so thankful that he was always looking after me.

I saw Marshall head for the door and I impulsively asked, "Master?"

He stopped and turned around. "Yes, Brand?"

"Can you let Jeremy out of his cage . . . please, sir?" I didn't think it was fair to have him being punished when I so obviously was rewarded for the same act.

"Yes, I can do that for you."

"Thank you, Master." I looked up into Chase McIntyre's light gray eyes as they bore down on me. "And thank you, Master."

"I'm not your Master," he said flatly.

"You are just as much my Master as that man," I said.

"He owns you."

"He owns the rights to me, but you own my ass, Master."

He smiled a huge toothy smile and said, "Is that right?"

"That's exactly right, Master. I've never been so dominated and . . ."

"And what?"

I blushed with embarrassment and said, "And satisfied by one man before." It cost me a lot to admit this, but I was feeling especially close to him and eager for his continued attention. "And that's why you are my Master."

"Well, we may feel that way, but let's keep that to ourselves, huh?"

"Yes, Master." I would never want to hurt Marshall's feelings, so I vowed to keep this secret, although I was pretty sure that all of my fellow Servants and my Master knew what was going on between Chase and myself.

CHAPTER ELEVEN

M aster informed us that night that the team had a pre-season game tomorrow and that we would be needed at the stadium. This news brought a lot of excitement with it, but also a lot of questions. Of course, we weren't allowed to ask them, and Master didn't seem to be willing to tell us anything more on his own, so we would just have to wait and see what tomorrow would bring.

Between the game tomorrow and Jeremy and me getting caught fucking, the four of us had a lot to discuss when Master went to bed. He had informed us that he needed his strength and stamina tomorrow, so he would give us the night off.

I quickly told Braden and Alex to come to our room. We all relaxed on the bed while Jeremy told the story of our indiscretion. Alex and Braden laughed and made crude comments to each of us during the story. We all laughed easily. They were very curious about our punishments and Jeremy couldn't wait to hear what mine had been since he didn't know either.

I told them what had happened and Alex said, "Well, that's not a very bad punishment."

Jeremy echoed, "It's almost a reward."

"It was. That's why I asked Master to free you from the cage. I felt really guilty."

"Man, Chase McIntyre can't get enough of you, can he?" Braden asked.

"To be honest, I feel the same way about him. Don't tell

Master," I confided in my fellow Servants.

Jeremy turned to Alex and Braden and said, "You guys haven't fucked around?"

"Oh, yeah. We blew each other in the shower," Alex said.

"Don't get caught," I warned them and started to laugh.

We started to talk about what would happen at the game tomorrow, but none of us had a clue, so it was all wild conjecture at this point. We decided to go to bed so that we were fresh for whatever would happen the next day. I turned off the lights after Alex and Braden went to their rooms and crawled into bed with Jeremy. That night I dreamed of Giants stadium as the gates of heaven, filled with thousands of big handsome burly men waiting for me to enter.

I woke with a great sense of excitement and couldn't wait to get the day started. Jumping into the shower, I scrubbed myself clean, both inside and out, before getting dressed in some of the team apparel that Master had given us. I had purchased a Taylor jersey at Marshalls and put that on to wear to the game. Jeremy was in the shower, so I went down to the kitchen to grab a bowl of cereal.

Alex and Braden were both sitting around the island in the kitchen when I walked in. I was shocked to see them dressed up in dress pants, dress shirts, and ties.

"Hey, guys. You guys are really formal today."

Alex looked down at what he was wearing and back up, "We weren't sure what to wear, so we decided on looking our best."

"It's hard to know what to wear when we aren't sure what we are going to be doing," I commented, pouring the cereal into a bowl and grabbing a spoon out of the drawer, never once thinking about going up and putting on my dress clothes.

"You are all very presentable for the game today."

We all turned to see that Master had just entered the room. He was dressed in Khakis and a golf shirt with the team logo on it. He headed to the fridge and grabbed the carton of milk, pouring some in my bowl as I held it steady.

"Thank you, Master."

"No problem. Where's Jeremy?"

"He was just getting out of the shower, so he should be here in a couple of minutes."

"We have to go in about a half hour."

"Yes, sir," we all said in unison. Just then, Jeremy walked in wearing Master's jersey just like me.

"You want us to change into dress clothes, Master?" I asked.

"No, you're good. None of you will be wearing clothes for long, anyway." Master's eyes sparkled with devious intent.

My crotch tingled in anticipation of what was to come, and the four of us looked at each other questioningly. We were all excited to get out of the house again and to especially see the stadium. We took two big SUVs, Master and his bodyguards in one and the Servants and one bodyguard in the other. We talked excitedly about seeing the other players and watching Master work.

I saw signs for East Rutherford, New Jersey and knew that we were there. Alex and Braden had no clue that a football team in New York played ball in New Jersey, so Jeremy and I scoffed at them. MetLife Stadium was huge as we drove up to the players' entrance. Security checked Master's ID in the car ahead of us and I saw his arm point at us out of the window. The security guard said something through the window and waved us both inside.

The two SUVs parked beside each other and we unloaded. I felt like it was the first day of school and I had no idea of what the building contained or what I was supposed to do once inside. Fortunately for me, I had three other friends with me in the same boat, and that really did make it better.

We walked down into a cement tunnel that put us into the underground section of the stadium. We went through security twice more, at the second one stopping to get our pictures made and receiving access badges to wear. I was surprised to see that Master had all four of our drivers' licenses with him to prove who we were. I guess I had never thought about it, but The Service probably sent him all kinds of paperwork on us.

We took an elevator down a couple of floors to the locker room. Master had to use his ID to get access for the elevator and the floor. I was glad to see that he was so well protected from the fans here at work.

The locker room was connected to a glass-enclosed weight room, and some of the players were pumping iron and running on treadmills to get ready for the game. We walked past the weight room and into the locker room. It was gorgeous, with thick carpet done in the team colors, which were red, white, and blue. The wood lockers and the benches looked like some type of walnut and there were big screen TVs on the walls, as well as motivational sayings painted prominently.

It smelled like a locker room, or at least, what I remembered my high school locker room smelled like—a heady combination of sweat, feet, and musky male pheromones. My ass itched at the thought of what might happen here and my heart beat faster at the possibilities. Master showed us his locker and then ours. Each player had one locker for himself and one for a Servant.

"Alex, you will use my Servant's locker. Brand, Chase said you could use his extra locker. Jeremy and Braden, you can use Peters and Jackson's, because they don't have Servants yet." Master pointed out all of the lockers and I noticed that Chase's locker was already full of his things. He must have been here already, but I had not seen him yet.

"What should we do now, Master?" Jeremy asked.

"Undress, of course," he said with a chuckle. "You guys are this morning's entertainment."

A bolt of fear ran through my body like I had been given an electric shock. *Entertainment* was not a word that I enjoyed hearing very much. Just then some other players came in, followed by their Servants. The players were sizing us up, the lust and need obvious on all of their faces. Their Servants were also sizing us up, judgment clearly defined on their faces.

One particularly nice marked guy came over to the group of us while Master went to get taped up. "Hey, fellas!" He was a light-skinned black guy with a really vibrant blue mark on his face. He was tall and skinny like a basketball player, with a nice big smile. "I'm Gene. You guys are Taylor's new Servants?"

"Yes, we are," I answered, holding out my hand to shake. "I'm Brand and this is Jeremy, Alex, and Braden." I pointed to each of them in kind.

"Hi." He shook hands with each of us. Afterwards, he stepped back and asked, "Did your Master tell you what is about to happen?"

"No," Alex whispered.

Gene chuckled and asked, "Do you want to know?"

"Yes," we all said with relief.

"Coach Mancini won't let the players fuck around until after the game, so to get the players' juices flowing, so to speak, he asks the Servants to perform right after his motivational speech."

"Perform?" I asked.

"Have an orgy with each other, basically," Gene said with a smile.

"How many Servants are there?" Braden asked.

"We had six before Taylor went out and got four of you at

one time, so now there are ten of us." Gene winked and said, "It's going to be a big pile!"

"I'll say," Alex said, licking his lips in anticipation.

More players and Servants were coming into the locker room now, and the circle around us was getting bigger as the other Servants were joining us.

Gene continued, "The players watch us, of course, and then if they like what they see, they can bid on us for after the game."

"Bid on us?" I repeated him as a query.

"To be with them. They put slips of paper in our Master's helmets and the top two in dollar amounts get to celebrate with us after the game. Half the money goes to charity and the other half goes to your Master," Gene continued.

One of the other Servants butted in. "Don't forget about the Fan Favorite . . ."

We looked from him to Gene. "One of the fans is selected each week for a locker room experience and he gets to put a slip of paper in one of the helmets to automatically get to fuck with one of us. This is known as the Fan Favorite. We are not allowed to tell him who our Master is, so that he doesn't just vote for his favorite player."

This was all news to me, and I immediately looked around the room at who my options were. I assumed that Chase would bid pretty high for me, so I would have to fuck with one other player. Fortunately for me, most of them were big and beefy—just my type. Some of the players were unattractive, and the linemen were overweight, but on the whole they radiated sexual energy and the room was buzzing with it.

"Thanks for the heads-up, Gene," I told my new friend.

"No problem. One of the older Servants told me for my first game, so I think it was only fair to pay it forward."

Just then the room got quiet, and I saw that Coach had walked into the middle of the room and was getting ready to address the players. Several players came in from different rooms, and I saw Chase McIntyre slide into the back. He searched the room for me before meeting my gaze. He smirked heavily at me, his eyes blazing from across the room towards me. I smiled at him and felt that familiar tingle in my crotch bloom into a full bonfire. My cock was already hard, like it had been almost constantly since I stepped out of my cage into this assignment.

Coach Mancini started to talk, and Gene indicated for us to undress. We went to our lockers and hung up our clothes as we took them off. We were soon naked and waiting for the Coach to finish. We took the time to introduce ourselves to our fellow Servants. John, Charlie, and Isaiah were tall and skinny. Sherman and Chris were short and skinny. Douglas was short and muscular, like Jeremy. I was the only one of my type, which was tall and thicker. I thought of it as an advantage to stand out.

Coach Mancini finished up his speech and then said, "Guys, I want to introduce you to our Fan of the Week!"

A six-foot-three-inch, thick-bodied construction worker walked into the locker room from the open door. He wore a sleeveless shirt, jeans, and black construction boots. He had some big-ass biceps with one small tattoo that I couldn't quite make out. His brown hair hung out slightly from a baseball cap, which he wore slightly off-center. A diamond stud earring and a full beard completed his look. He was absolutely jaw-dropping masculinity and I wanted him to pick me to fuck more than anything. I immediately envisioned him and Chase taking turns fucking me.

"This is Bill from Yonkers. Bill, these are your favorite players!" Coach yelled and left the room.

There was a lot of cheering and whooping from the players. The players greeted Bill fondly and surrounded him for a minute or so. Then they backed away to the edges of the room, clearing a space in the middle of the locker room for us. Led by the older Servants, we all walked into the circle. Gene was carrying two bottles of lube which he sat down on one of the wooden benches.

The four of us waited for our cues. It wasn't a long wait. Charlie closed the gap between him and me with one long stride, planting his lips on mine firmly. I saw that he was trying to take control, so I fixed that right away. Crushing my mouth to his, I pushed back on him, taking over the advantage. I looked to the side and saw my friends in similar sexual entanglements, and a quick glance at the players showed me that we had their total focus.

I put my hands on either side of Charlie's blond crew-cut head and pushed him down to his knees. I saw the look in his blue eyes as I pushed him down in front of me and it was a mixture of submission and the lustful need to be dominated.

Holding the back of his head, I pointed my hard cock at his mouth before slapping him across the face with it. His blond chinstrap tickled the sensitive skin of my member and I heard small grunts and chuckles come from the players. Charlie opened his mouth, and I fed my cock to him. He was a very good cocksucker, but I wanted to fuck him so that the players would get fired up for the game.

Once my cock was hard and wet, I pulled it out of his mouth and bent him over the wooden bench. I could see that a lot of the other couples were taking turns and blowing each other, but I had already decided on a game plan, and that was not it. I handed him a folded towel so that the bench didn't hurt him right before I spread his ass cheeks and planted my face inside them. He had a nice tight asshole, and I enjoyed rimming and tongue-fucking him. The heat blossomed on his light skin, and I slapped his ass cheeks just to make them even redder.

Whispering to him as I lay my body across his back, I

asked, "You ready, Charlie?"

"Fuck yes," he confirmed to me. I could hear more than just the theater of it in his voice. He was genuinely turned on.

I grabbed the bottle of lube and squirted some on my cock head and rubbed it on. I squirted a generous amount on the top of his lily-white ass and let it run over his puckered hole. As soon as it was over his rosebud, I slipped two of my slickened fingers inside him.

Charlie sucked in his breath hard and instinctively pulled away from my fingers. "Don't you fucking pull away from me," I growled.

"Oh, fuck!" one player yelled.

"He's trying to be the man, Taylor!" another one shouted.

"That's my boy!" Marshall yelled back. I glanced over to see that Chase was urging me on by holding up a fist and shaking it. He mouthed the word, *Go!*

I finger-blasted Charlie with some force before hunching over him and sliding my cock inside him. The head cleared his anal ring, and I buried my shaft inside him up to the nuts. His asshole wasn't tight, but it wasn't loose, either. I got the impression that his Master fucked him often, but not with a dick as big as my own.

Charlie moaned in response to my deep-dicking. I put my hands on the handles of his hips and pulled his ass back as far onto my big pole as it could possibly go. And then I fucking tore him a new asshole. I fucked Charlie's ass as fast and furiously as I could. When I came, I roared with my climax, pulled out of his sweet ass, grabbed my cock by the base, and held it steady as I shot thick strands of hot cum arching in the air that landed on Charlie's back.

All sound was muted as I pumped my cock and milked the last bit of cum out of me. When my heart stopped racing, the noise came back to me and I could hear the players laughing and cheering. I was still breathing deep lungsful of air when

I lifted Charlie off the bench and checked to make sure he was all right.

"Better than alright." Charlie beamed at me. "That was fucking awesome!"

A bell rang somewhere, and the players all went back to their lockers to make their bids. Helmets were lined up for the ten of us. Since our Master had four Servants, they used different colored helmets of his and put our names on each one.

Gene signaled us to go into the showers. We followed him and the other Servants in.

"We're not supposed to be out there when they place the bids," Charlie told us.

"Plus, we have to get cleaned up for them to enjoy us after the game," Sherman added.

"Not like we don't know the outcome already," Gene said with a snort. "That was some show you put on out there, Brand." Gene looked at me with a mixture of admiration and wonder.

"I'm not sure it was a show," Jeremy said as the ten of us stood in a circle under the warm water from the showers. "He fucked the shit out of me last night the same exact way."

I blushed with embarrassment at their words. "What? It wasn't anything special . . ."

"Like hell!" Isaiah said. "You fucked him like a NOMAR, didn't he Charlie?"

Charlie had yet to stop gazing at me. I could tell that he was enamored with me, or at least my fucking ability. "It was a great fuck. I only wish we could do it again and I could be under you and watch you destroying my ass." His voice was breathy, like he was trying to entice me again.

"Not happening, Charlie. We're getting ready to get fucked by some big bruisers, and you better hope they win, because there is nothing worse than getting anger-fucked by a filthy football player," Gene said, matter-of-factly.

I personally was excited by the visual that Gene's words had created in my head, but I kept my mouth closed, not knowing what it was really like.

"Not like we're going to make any money for our Masters today," Douglas said. "Not with Brand competing against us."

"That's bullshit," I said while soaping my crotch. "None of those NOMARs want to fuck with me. They like watching Charlie take me, is all." I wasn't sure about this, but was trying to make it sound good.

John spoke for the first time. "You would be surprised. Nothing turns them on like that fucking display you just put on . . ."

"Why?" I asked.

"They want to dominate the dominant," Alex informed us, like we were idiots.

It reminded me of what McIntyre had said to me after he caught me fucking Jeremy, right before he gave me the fuck of my life . . .

"Exactly!" Gene said. "If they can dominate the guy that dominates others, then they are king of the world."

I didn't know whether this pop-psychological theory was accurate or not, but I knew that I would find out soon enough.

CHAPTER TWELVE

When we exited the showers, the players were gone, so we dressed in a weird silence. Gene and the other more experienced Servants showed us up to a suite where we could watch the game. Our team had played well through the first three quarters and had the lead, when Gene announced it was time to leave.

Once back in the locker room, Gene filled us in on what was going to happen. "I have a list of the bids for each of us, and we will be secured in the player's locker who bid the most for us. Once the players come into the locker room, your assignments and amounts will be announced."

My head was swimming and I had a lot of questions.

"Once you have fucked with your two or three guys, you are free to leave with your Masters. Here are the assignments for the end of the game — John is assigned to Valesquez, Charlie is assigned to Carter, Sherman you have Nichols, Isaiah has Linzer, Douglas gets Rahkimova, Chris gets White, Brand has Peters, Alex gets Forest, Jeremy is assigned to McNally, and Braden gets Mooney."

"Peters bid the highest?" Sherman asked in disbelief.

"You know we don't know the bids," Gene said.

"What's wrong with Peters?" I asked, suddenly concerned because that was who I was assigned to. I was still a little in shock that McIntyre had not won me. I also noticed that Master was not one of the names called, even though he made the most money on the team.

"Nothing," Gene said. "He's a rookie and good looking, so

all of us wanted to try him out."

"Usually rookies are cheap and don't bid," Chris said.

"Well, he did." Gene ended the discussion. "Let's get undressed and lube ourselves." We all went to our lockers and stripped down. Some of the guys on this team were huge, so I generously greased my little hole in anticipation.

A short guy wearing khakis and a knit shirt with the team logo on it restrained us to our player's locker. I was amazed at how the handcuffs were made of some type of Kevlar material, comfortable, but entirely inescapable. Some of us were hung in a straight line, bound at the top and bottom. I was hung in a cross, with my arms and legs all separated. Jeremy was hung facing inward with his ass in the air. All of us had ball gags strapped to our heads so that we could not speak.

While I hung there, I had some time to think. I was curious to know who Peters was, since I was unfamiliar with him. I hoped that Chase McIntyre was my second or third player. I wondered what it would be like to be under some of these players who were so big. I also wondered how Master would deal with me being fucked right in front of him, or whether he would he even care.

I could hear some of the cheering from the game when the door was opened by different people. The team, or the players, had made sure that there was security that watched us as we hung in the locker room. I could just imagine what bad things could have happened if an asshole fan got access to that locker room with us hanging there for them like naked stockings filled with presents on Christmas Day.

There was a sudden eruption of sound, and then people started to stream into the locker room. Each player reported to their locker, and the ones who had us hanging there for them were very excited. A lot of the players slapped us on the ass, pinched our nipples, or pulled on our cocks.

Peters arrived at his locker and grinned from ear to ear. He was a big boy—six-four and over three hundred pounds of sheer muscle and bulk. He had hair cut short that was dark brown with a matching one-day beard. His oval face was kind, and his smile was infectious.

"Hey, Buddy," he said excitedly, smacking me on the cheek of my face. Normally, that would not have hurt, but the ball gag had my cheek stretched wide, and it pinched me when he smacked me.

I knew I couldn't say anything understandable, so I didn't even attempt it.

Peters had turned and was celebrating with some of the players. Chase McIntyre came into the locker room, and I saw that he spotted me right away. He headed straight for me, a look of sorrow on his face.

Instead of coming right up to me, Chase veered to the side of me at the last second. I realized that his locker was right next to Peters'.

Chase approached me, bent to my ear, and whispered, "Sorry. I'm saving my money." He pulled back, and I saw how miserable he looked. I wanted to talk to him, but all I had were my eyes, so I tried to tell him that it was okay.

We were all distracted as Taylor raised his voice and spoke, "Well, guys. That was a great game for us!" The players cheered. "And now it is time to celebrate." More cheering.

Master grabbed a helmet and started to read the bids. Most of them were a couple of hundred dollars each. He saved his four helmets for last. Braden had three bids, all five hundred dollars and over. Alex had the same. Jeremy had three bids, one of them a thousand dollars.

Taylor picked up his helmet with my name on it and told the crowd that I had two bids. I was immediately very disappointed that I hadn't been able to entice three players. Master continued, "Brand's second bid is Deal, who bid fifteen hundred dollars." This drew a huge cacophony of sound and motion from the players, centered on one guy. This must have been Deal. He was huge, easily six-five and over three hundred pounds. Leave it to me to get two tackles interested in me . . .

"And the highest bid was by Peters who bid . . ." Master paused for dramatic effect. "Two thousand five hundred dollars for Brand!"

The room erupted with sound. Peters was swarmed by the players in all states of undress. He was soon buried under a massive mound of bodies. Most of the players were saying things like, "Don't blow all of your money in one shot, rookie!" or "Blowing a load to blow a load, rookie!"

Master waited until the yelling stopped and said, "And of course, the Fan Favorite today goes to Brand!" Bill hunched over from the whoops and backslaps from the players. I was shocked at this additional compliment, but my crotch caught fire shortly afterwards when I realized that I was going to get fucked by Bill the construction worker.

Master walked over and told me how proud he was of me and then saw how miserable his friend was. He smacked my ass and said, "Me and Mac will see you at home when you are done. Won't we, Chase?"

Chase put on a half-smile and said, "Yep. That's what we will do. We'll see you later."

I moved my head up and down to signal my agreement. I implored Chase with my eyes to not be upset, but I could see that I was having no effect. All of the players were getting down to business now, and the room went silent. A lot of the players stripped and headed to the showers. The smell of the locker room quickly became strong. I had never been in a room of 30-plus guys who were sweaty and muddy, and the smell and all the skin was almost more than I could take.

When Peters began to strip in front of me, I couldn't help but get hard. He knew what he was doing, taking his time and keeping me waiting. My cock filled with blood, hardened, and then started to point at the sky. Peters had a great body, big and thick with a hairy chest and a nice thick cock with a purple head.

He undid the Velcro from my cuffs and pushed my shoulders down. I knew what that meant, so I lowered to my knees. Peters undid my gag and threw it on the floor. I realized immediately that my mouth was still going to be stretched, just using a different gag. Grabbing the base of his big cock with one hand, I guided it to my mouth with the other. He tasted like sweat and musk, and I let him fill my mouth up with his manhood. I didn't have to suck long, because within seconds he had a raging hard-on that was so hot it threatened to burn my lips.

Peters moaned and then grabbed me under the arms and lifted me onto a nearby bench. Hunching over me, he bent me in half, holding my legs down by my head with one hand while he fed his cock into my hole with the other.

That purple cockhead blasted through my anal ring, stretching me wide open as he filled my ass with his meat. Once he had slid in up to his nuts, he arched his back and held it there while I used my ass muscles to squeeze his thick stick.

"Is it worth twenty-five hundred dollars, Peters?" one of the players asked.

Peters opened his eyes, sighed, and said, "Fuck! You gotta feel how tight this ass is." He looked down at me, undulating his hips to keep himself throbbing inside of me. "When I saw you dominating that other Servant, I knew I had to have you—to dominate you just like you did to that other guy."

I guess the boys were right. "Why don't you get started fucking that tight ass, then?" I asked sarcastically, so that the others could hear.

My smart mouth made the room erupt in laughter and cat calls.

Someone yelled, "Even the rookie Servant is giving the rookie shit!"

Peters's face dropped, so I rallied to cover. "Peter's big cock is filling me up so completely that I can't wait for him to start tearing me up!"

He looked down at me in surprise, and I saw the huge grin spread over his face again and knew he was okay.

"Fuck yeah!" he roared as he began to fuck me with all the finesse of a lumberjack competing in the Timbersport Competition on ESPN. I thought he was going to saw me in half, as he literally hunched his body over mine and rammed his big cock into me repeatedly. I did enjoy his big 300-plus pounds bearing down on me and I grabbed hold of each of his biceps as I rode his thrusts.

My cock was still rock-hard, and the fact that it was constantly being stroked by his hairy belly sent me over the edge of my climax. I shot ropes of pearly white cum into his dark hair as I rode the wooden bench underneath this bull. My ass muscles clamped down on his cock, pushing him to the brink of his climax.

"Fuck me!" he roared from deep in his chest.

I saw movement out of the corner of my eye and looked over to see Chase McIntyre. He was just finished getting dressed and glanced quickly at me before putting his gym bag on his shoulder and leaving. He looked so unhappy and I felt bad for him. I would see him tonight and I promised myself to make it all better for him.

Peters continued to hunch over me and work his legs and hips to milk every last drop of his cum into me. Finally his rhythm fell apart and he pulled out of me, bringing his sloppy cock up to my mouth to clean off.

"That was so fucking worth it," he told me, as I sucked some remaining cum from his big hose. "Taylor is a lucky man to have you as his Servant."

Pulling his cock out of my hot mouth, I said, "You were pretty fantastic, too, Peters. You can fuck me anytime."

He smiled at me and pointed over to Deal's locker.

I hurried over to where Deal was waiting. He was already naked, and I saw I was facing another big guy, even bigger than Peters, as a matter of fact. When I stood in front of him, I saw his cock for the first time. It was unlike any I had ever encountered before. His cock was shorter than average, but had a tremendous girth. It looked almost swollen. It was so bizarre looking.

"You like that big thick cock?" he asked, his voice husky with lust for me.

"Yes, sir."

"Good, because I'm getting ready to stretch that little asshole of yours out with it."

"Yes, sir." I was frightened that I was not going to be able to take his dick. Even if I got him inside me somehow, how in the hell was I going to be able to handle him fucking me with it?

I watched as Deal stood up, spread some towels down on the thick carpet in front of his locker. He had a great ass, covered lightly with brown hair and his thigh muscles were some of the largest I had ever seen. He sat back down on the wooden bench and pointed at his cock.

Deal was not attractive, but he was so good-natured that his smile lit up his face and made him more attractive than he normally would have been. He was one of those guys that people were drawn to because of their personality. I liked him already, even though I barely knew him. His chest was broad with a smattering of brown hair between his pecs over his breastbone. He had a gut that hung over his crotch, causing me to briefly start to daydream about what it was going to be like to be under his massive bulk.

I snapped myself out of my sexual fantasy and dropped to

my knees in front of him. I grabbed hold of his unusual cock, licking up the sides of his enormously thick shaft to his cock-head that looked like a cork plugging a piece of PVC pipe. He tasted sweaty, and I licked the salt from his skin.

Deal held my head in place as I unhinged my jaw to suck his big member into my mouth. It certainly felt like it. He stretched my mouth like no one I had ever blown before, and I knew this was just a foretaste of the stretching that was going to take place in my ass.

Deal's cock seemed to be the same, whether hard or soft, so I was a little surprised when he told me he was ready for me to lube him. He had a huge tub of Vaseline that he asked me to use on him.

"Don't be stingy. You're gonna wanna use as much of this as you can," he told me, starting to laugh.

Once I had him properly greased, he turned me around and lubed my asshole. I knew that I had Peter's load in there, as well as the lube I had used before, but I guessed it didn't matter, because Deal was going to need all the lube I could stand.

I hoped he was going to want to fuck me doggy-style, because that would be the easiest position to be in to handle his girth. After his big chubby fingers explored my hole, he spun me back towards him.

"Why don't you have a seat here in my lap?" He smiled down at me.

He was making sure he picked the position that left me the most vulnerable to him. I tried to turn around so I could back into his lap, but he turned me back to face him.

"No, little one! I am the one in charge now," he growled.

I appreciated his command of me and my cock started to harden as my balls tingled with electric currents. Straddling his big legs, I let him guide me where he wanted me to be. Deal wanted me against him—pressed against his big chest.

He hugged me to him, tightly. I felt like a hot blanket had been thrown around me, like the towel they give you at a barber shop to open your pores.

When Deal released his grip on me, he reached between his legs and aimed his monster-wide cock at my hole. I could tell that he was enjoying watching my face. I tried not to wince as I felt him against me. It was like sitting on a pylon on the pier. I slowly tried to press down onto him.

Deal shook his head from side to side, smiled broadly, and said, "No, little one. You are not in charge here. I've done this many times and I know what is best . . ."

I had no choice, so I acquiesced to him.

Deal reached down behind me and used his thick fingers to spread my puckered hole wide open. He held it there, open and unnatural, until he readjusted and slid into me. I immediately saw stars, and red tongues of fire flew up my spine and radiated out from my asshole.

He did know what he was doing, because he didn't stop sliding himself into me until he was all the way inside. He must have known that it would be harder for me if he had gone slowly or stopped and tried to let me get used to it. I had never been stretched like this before, and the fact that the rest of my ass was not reaping any of the benefits from it was the most unusual part of it.

Deal rocked us back and forth, causing my drum-tight asshole to move up and down on him slightly. He bent to my ear and whispered in his big booming voice, "When I saw you fucking Charlie earlier, it was so fucking hot that I knew I had to have you in this position."

"Why, sir?" I asked, feeling the echo of my words in my asshole.

"Because nothing brings me greater pleasure than impaling an alpha male on this thick cock and watching his eyes roll back in his head."

"Or scream at the top of his lungs, sir?"

"Exactly!"

"You think I'm an alpha male, sir?"

"I know you are. I watched you fuck earlier, and I've seen how you have tamed McIntyre."

I was stunned. "What, sir?"

"McIntyre has been a real ass-hound since he got here and now, since your arrival, he suddenly is not . . ."

I flushed, as much from his words as from the constant pressure he was putting on my asshole.

"He's even trying to save up money, so he can afford you as his Servant when your contract is over with Taylor."

"What?" This was news to me, and my heart swelled to know that Chase felt this way about me.

"Now that I'm sitting here reaming you out, I see why he's so obsessed with you. It's a nice ass."

"Thanks, Deal. Your cock is pretty exciting, as well."

"Well, now that we've stroked each other, let's get to it!" He wrapped his big arms around my back and lifted us from the bench. I clung to his big body as he knelt on the towels on the carpet and lowered my back to the floor. He bent my legs back and I held them up against my chest as he laid his 300 pounds on top of me.

"Fuck me, sir."

"I'm going to give you the ride of your life."

Deal began to give me an awesome fucking that involved him just moving his hips in a circle, slow and methodical. I don't think his cock moved in and out of me more than an inch, but it was a fantastic fuck and one I would never forget.

Chapter Thirteen

Once in the car, the four of us Taylor Servants talked excitedly about our experiences and gossiped about the different players. They enjoyed hearing me tell my stories, especially about the Fan Favorite. I relived it for them.

Bill, the construction worker, was a little on the drunk side by the time I finished with Deal. My ass was full of cum and burning from two hard fucks. Even though Bill was pretty hot, I really just wanted to get a shower. My mind was changed when I saw him naked. His body was phenomenal, and he kept his construction boots on, which I personally enjoyed.

He let me run my hands over his chiseled chest, his rock-hard abs, and his bazooka-sized biceps. I must have been mesmerized, because he had to put a rough hand to my face to get my attention. He wanted me to lie down on the bench, and then he face-fucked me while I held onto his ripped thighs. His cock was average in every way, but it was connected to one of the most gorgeous bodies I had ever seen, so I didn't care so much.

Bill smelled of beer and sweat, but tasted musky and delicious. I sucked him up hard before he told me to get on all fours. He gave me a serious fucking from behind, using my hips to move my ass back and forth on his cock. Normally, I would have enjoyed this position at the end of a long fuck session, but Bill's assets were hidden from me in this position, so I was a little bummed.

When Bill got close to his climax, he held me still and

fucked fast and hard into me, his balls slapping against my own. He built the pace until he eventually exploded inside me. I could feel the cum running down my legs as he churned it out of me.

He continued to thrust, whispering to me even as he kept going, "I know I'm only supposed to fuck you once, but I need to go again, so don't let on . . ."

"Yes, sir," I responded, knowing that I fired his engine, even as I said it.

"Do you want to pick the position?" he asked as he pulled out of my sloppy hole. I was surprised that he would let me.

"I'm kinda a mess, sir. Would you like to shower?" I turned around to face him.

"Sure."

I made sure I raised my voice slightly, "Maybe you can bust a nut in the shower, sir."

He smiled at my smokescreen and I motioned for him to sit down. He did, and I pulled his boots off, making sure to smell each one of them before placing it to the side. I pulled his socks off and repeated the process. His feet were his least attractive feature, being skinny, white, and veiny, with toenails that needed trimming. I could see why he kept his boots on.

I stood up and grabbed him by the hand, leading him to the showers. I pushed him down onto one of the benches in the shower area, turned on the water, and dropped between his legs. Sucking him, I reveled in the taste of his cummy cock. I also loved looking up at him while I pleasured him.

When Bill was hard again, I sat down in his lap, impaling myself on his cock, just like I had with Deal, but this time, I was the aggressor. I took Bill's handsome face in my hands and planted my mouth on his. My lips crushed his and my tongue entered his mouth, hungrily searching for his own. The stale taste of beer was in his saliva, but I didn't care.

He broke my lip lock and said, "Hey, man, I like fucking

your tight little ass, but I'm not marked."

"You don't have to be, man. There are NOMARs that like to be fucked, who like to suck dick, who eat ass, who get fisted. I just thought you wanted the whole experience."

"No problem. I'm just gonna fuck your sweet ass once more and I'll be happy."

"Sounds good."

Bill stood with me in his lap, planted his feet firmly on the shower tiles, and fucked me while he stood. I rose and fell on his cock as his hips sent me sliding up his shaft and gravity pulled me back down. I held onto his big arms, pinching his little tight nipples occasionally.

Bill's second climax was just as forceful as his first. He planted my back onto the tiled wall and fucked his last few thrusts into me from below as his upper body held me in place. Afterwards, he thanked me for a great fuck and left to high-five the few remaining players left in the locker room.

I showered with the other Servants as they slowly trickled in. Some of them had finished earlier, so they were already gone. Charlie was still left and he whispered that he couldn't wait until the next game to repeat our performance. I could tell that he meant it, seeing the need in his eyes and hearing the desperation in his voice. We said goodbye and headed out to the car with Master's security guard in tow.

Chase and Master were happy to see us when the car dropped us off at the house. I was exhausted, and fortunately Master gave us permission to take a nap. They were both tired from the game as well, so all six of us went to sleep for a while. Master came to each of our rooms and handed us *Aleve*. Swallowing the pain pills, I reminded myself how lucky I was to be with this man who cared for us so well and made a mental note to myself to pay him back in my own special way later.

I woke an hour and a half later and tiptoed out of the

bedroom, trying not to wake Jeremy. Going downstairs, I found Master and McIntyre making dinner in the kitchen.

"Hi, Master, McIntyre," I said, not yet revealing that I called them both by that title.

"Brand." Chase smoldered with his deep voice.

"You're the first one up, Brand. I thought you might need to sleep some more," Master commented.

"I'm good with a quick nap, Master. If I sleep longer, I may not sleep tonight."

"You may not sleep tonight anyway," Chase threatened.

I felt my face flush, and my words smoldered back at him, "I would gladly give up sleep for that reason, sir."

"Only if Taylor doesn't need you." Chase turned to his best friend and raised an eyebrow.

"I'm good. I think I'm going to put Jeremy through his paces tonight. Anyway, after Brand rode Deal, you're probably the only one of us that will give him any pleasure tonight!"

"True enough," McIntyre said, starting to laugh.

"He's a big fucker," I added.

"Sure is! Have you ever seen a cock like that in all your . . . travels, Brand?"

"Fuck, no! I thought it was going to fucking split me in half."

We all laughed.

"He better not have," McIntyre said, glaring at me.

"He didn't," I said, defensively. "But he sure tried."

"I'm also going to try," McIntyre admitted.

"After dinner, boys," Master said, as he returned to chopping vegetables.

"Can I help you, Master?"

"You like to cook?"

"Yes, sir."

"I'll let you finish these so I can work on the pasta."

After a dinner of plank-grilled salmon and pasta primavera, the six of us watched *World War Z* in Master's theatre room. I was amazed that he had a theatre in his home and again that he was such a celebrity that he could get a copy of a movie that was still in theaters. It was amazing to me how the rich and famous lived.

As soon as the movie ended, Master turned up the lights, and I saw that Braden and Alex were both asleep in their chairs. Jeremy had been told that he was spending the night with Master, so he seemed wired for it.

McIntyre turned to his friend and asked, "Are you sure you're okay with Brand spending the night with me, Taylor?"

"Absolutely, Chase! I've got my hands full with Jeremy here. You two go have fun."

"Thanks, man!" McIntyre grinned broadly. We stood up, and I woke up Alex and Braden, winking at Jeremy as I did. Chase and I walked past Master's chair on the way to the stairs.

"Oh, Brand," he said, grabbing my arm as I passed him. I turned back towards him, and he pulled me down until his mouth was at my ear. "Thanks for taking care of him. You are a miracle-worker."

"You're welcome, Master. And thank you for everything that you do for me and for all of us. I really appreciate it."

He smiled at me and let me go. As Chase and I hit the stairs, we could hear Master asking Jeremy if he was ready to go also.

Jeremy's response was, "Or we could start right here, Master."

I smiled to myself as I watched the man whom I considered my true Master walk up the stairs in front of me. My cock was filling with blood and my balls were sparking with tingling sensations. I couldn't wait for him to be inside me.

He held the door to his bedroom open for me and closed it

behind us.

I immediately dropped into The Service Squat and said, "Master." My voice was heady with lust and husky with need.

He walked towards me and raised my head with a big hand under my chin. He hooked a rough thumb into the side of my mouth, pointing my gaze right at his. Chase's light-grey eyes shone in the darkened room like the moon in the night sky. "I didn't like seeing you with those other players."

My heart stopped. He was mad at me, and I had not seen that coming. "I'm sorry, Master."

"You have nothing to apologize for."

Now I was confused. "Master?"

"I didn't like it, not because you were with them, but because I had no control over it."

"And if you did, Master, would you have stopped it?" This was way out of line for a Servant to ask or even to speak without being asked a question, but I was dying to know the answer, so I took the risk.

"No." I stared into his eyes and saw that he spoke the truth. "I was so proud of you when you were with the other Servants." This was the first I was hearing of this. "I wanted everyone there to know that you belonged to me, but you didn't, and that was what was upsetting to me."

"I belong to you, Master." He still had his thumb in the corner of my mouth, so I took the opportunity to suck on it. It was salty and tasted like the popcorn we had just eaten during the movie.

"Only in here." Chase's knees buckled for a second and then he caught himself. "Oh, fuck," he whispered, looking up to the ceiling.

"Then this is where we shall live, Master."

His lips formed into the smirk that I was starting to know so well.

"So, you liked the way I fucked Charlie, Master?"

"Fuck, yes! But tonight, you are going to follow my commands, or I'll have to punish you."

The thought of him punishing me both terrified and excited, so, of course, I desperately wanted his punishment. "Yes, sir." My mouth was dry and my heart was racing.

"Good, now let's see what we can do with that mouth of yours . . ." Chase pushed my mouth open with his thumb as he removed it. I kept it open. "Reach into my fly."

I followed his commands, reaching inside the fly of his shorts and pulling his big monster out. It was hot and throbbed in my hand. I tried to guide it into my mouth, but he pulled back from me. I looked up at him, questioningly.

"I didn't tell you to pull it out," he said, his voice blazing with lust.

Oh, so this is how it's going to go? "Shall I put it back in, Master?"

He swallowed hard, his cock still throbbing away in my hand. "No, suck the head. And that is one."

I smiled like a kid on Christmas morning. Licking and sucking Master's big cock-sickle, I swiped at his piss hole, catching his dew-like pre-cum on my tongue and swallowing it down. My mind was racing about what he meant by the phrase *and that is one.* I sucked hard on the head, momentarily running my tongue down along the shaft.

"No, Brand," Chase smirked. "That's two."

I pulled my tongue back. *He's counting how many times I disobey him?* I was absolutely turned-on by this man more than anyone I had ever met before. What would he do when he got to three? Three strikes and you're out?

Chase looked down at me and said, "Now, open wide."

I did, and he slid his shaft all the way into my mouth until his velvety-smooth cockhead was hitting against the back of my throat. My jaws stretched wide, virtually useless, but my lips and tongue worked overtime to pleasure him.

"Watch the teeth. That's three."

I waited for some type of punishment, but none came. What was Master up to?

Chase reached down and held my face with his palms. They were so hot against my skin. He rose onto the balls of his feet and began to thrust his hips forward and back, driving that magnificent organ into my throat over and over. I felt his cock twitch and I knew he was close.

"Swallow me, Brand." My Master moaned, arching his torso and raising up onto his toes.

My reward came seconds later, when his piss hole opened up and spewed forth the most delicious man-cream I had ever tasted. I swallowed quickly, but was overwhelmed with his size and the veracity of his ejaculation. I began to choke.

Chase pulled back his cock, except for the head, making it much easier for me to keep up with his delicious cum-fountain. He whispered, "Four." I wasn't sure how or when he was going to punish me, but I sure was giving him ammunition for it.

I held the base of his shaft with one hand so that I could clean up Master's cock. I did not miss a drop of his pearly-white man-juice and soon he was ready to go again. Chase McIntyre was a man with the virility of a jackrabbit, and I counted myself very lucky to have found him.

Chase's beautiful balls were swinging slowly back and forth beneath his big pole. I couldn't help but suck them into my still-hungry mouth, savoring their taste and smell. Rolling his big hairy balls around my mouth, I was in heaven until I heard his deep voice again.

"Five."

I spit his balls out and looked up at him. Master leaned down and pulled me into a standing position. We were face-to-face, our gazes locked onto each other.

"Are you ready for your punishment, Brand?" he asked with a smirk.

"Yes, Master." My whole body was ringing with anticipation.

"Well, you will just have to wait a little while longer . . ."

CHAPTER FOURTEEN

W*ait a little longer?*
I already thought I might explode with the sexual tension, and now Chase McIntyre was going to torture me by making me wait even longer. I wasn't sure what was about to happen, but I wanted it to happen right now.

"Take my shirt off, Brand." Chase's voice betrayed the fact that I had just blown him. His voice was just as lusty and laced with longing as it had been ten minutes ago.

"Yes, sir." I carefully grabbed the hem of his t-shirt and returned my eyes to his. I held his gaze as I lifted the shirt. He lifted his arms to help me, and suddenly his broad, muscular chest was right in front of me. I tweaked his rock-hard nipples as I passed them, removing the shirt off of his head and arms.

Chase shook his head from side to side with a fake look of disappointment on his face. "Six," he said, flatly. "Take off my shorts, Brand."

I looked down, hooking the elastic of his shorts with my thumbs and pushing them over his hips. His big cock pointed down as I slid the shorts down and off of him. Chase stepped out of them and over to the bed. Lying down on the bed, he dangled his feet over the edge.

"Take off my right sock, Brand." Master liked to wear those athletic socks that were gathered around his ankles. They were out of style for everyone but professional athletes. Chase McIntyre looked fucking hot in them, however. I pulled his right sock down and immediately ran my thumb down the bottom of his foot, tickling him.

He didn't laugh, but instead said, "Seven."

"Sorry, Master." I hung my head, figuring that I was disappointing him.

"Lick the bottom of my foot."

He didn't have to command me twice. I loved his feet almost as much as I loved his chest and cock, so I was all over it. I licked the entire bottom of his foot, before sucking on his heel and then his instep. Careful not to lick or suck his toes, I leaned back and awaited his next command.

"Very good. Now suck my toes and lick the top of my foot." I followed his command, enjoying his big toes in my mouth a lot more than I should have. When I was done, Master commanded me to repeat it all for his left foot. I tried to do the same good job on it, as I did on the right one. Master must have enjoyed it, because he couldn't stop smiling at me.

"Lick up the inside of my legs."

I immediately positioned myself to lick his ankle and move up the inside of his leg. When I got to his knee, I saw a nasty scar, ran my thumb over it and then my tongue. I looked up at him with a questioning look.

"I blew out my knee in college. Keep licking."

I put my head down and continued up his big thighs. Chase held his cock and balls out of my way, so I could lick his smooth inner thigh area. Repeating the line on the other side, I ended at his left ankle. Sitting up on my haunches, I waited for the next command like a well-behaved dog.

"That's nice, Brand." Master licked his lips and ordered, "Tongue in my bellybutton."

I leaned over him and dipped my tongue inside his deep little stomach hole. It thrilled me to taste him there, knowing that I hadn't before. Taking some initiative, I spit into his bellybutton and then flicked it out with the tip of my tongue.

"Now my chest, but not my nipples."

"My favorite, Master," I purred.

"More than this?" he smirked, poking me in the side with his meat sword.

"I could love nothing more than that, Master."

Chase laughed out loud, saying, "Nice cover. Get to work."

I took my time with his chest, memorizing every curve and nuance of his big burly, hairy, masculine chest. My tongue was dry and irritated, even as my cock hardened in response to how much I was enjoying it. I successfully avoided the first pink nubbin I encountered, but was unable to avoid the second one. Sucking it into my hot mouth, I licked it while I sucked it.

"Brand, you are the worst Servant for following directions . . ."

I was now hunched over him, but I hung my head in supplication again.

Chase reached up and brought my eyes back to his. "But, I am going to so enjoy punishing you for it." His smile lit up his handsome face, and his light-grey eyes sparkled with pleasure. "Eight."

He was killing me with this counting and waiting. Fortunately for me, Chase handed me a bottle of water from the nightstand, and I drank the whole thing.

"Now, the other one." I gave his second nipple the same treatment, feeling my cock trying to expand beyond its skin.

"Good." Chase reached up and fed his fingers slowly into my mouth. I grabbed his wrist, held it firm, and felicitated each one of his fingers, making sure that I licked his palm and the backs of his hands.

"Move up my arms." I followed his directive, and I found myself, once again, making a mental map of his body. I found every scrape and cut from the game, as well as old scars and bruises. I spent a lot of time on his big guns, loving the big bicep muscles and the veins that popped out on them.

Once I was finished, he said, "Armpits." The smirking

smile on his face was almost more than I could take. He obviously saw this as some kind of punishment, while I obviously saw it as a reward.

His armpits were normal-sized and full of dark hair. They didn't smell bad, but tasted like his deodorant. Master must have especially liked this, because he moaned and gyrated underneath me as I worked.

"Lie on top of me." This command threw me off my game more than any other. Usually it was Chase lying on top of me, and I tried to guess what he was up to, but to no avail. Crawling over him on all fours, I slowly lowered myself down until I was using him as a big hairy mattress. He held my sides with his rough hands so I wouldn't slip off of him. He was only slightly taller than me, so our heads were almost aligned. My painfully hard cock was smashed between our stomachs, and it was starting to give-off a tremendous amount of heat.

"I feel very close to you, Brand."

"And I you, Master."

"It's not like anything I have ever experienced before."

"Nor me, Master."

He stared at me in the dim light, snapped himself out of the moment, and said, "Lick my neck."

His neck was a thing of beauty, clean-shaven, thick and muscled without looking weird like a weightlifter's. I lifted my head above him so that I could dip down and cover all parts of his neck.

Softly, he said, "My ears." He had the smallest, cutest ears, and I sucked them into my mouth while running my tongue all over them with joy. Before I even knew what I was doing, I felt my tongue on his rough cheek and then my lips following them. I kissed him softly on one cheek and then the other.

"Nine," he said. Suddenly, he grabbed my face in both hands and said, "You are amazing, Brand. We are almost finished, and then you can have your punishment."

"Master," I said, breathily.

"I know you are looking forward to your punishment. I can feel your excitement punching into my stomach."

"Yes, sir."

He rolled me off of the top of him onto the mattress beside of him. Much to my surprise, I watched him roll over and fold his arms under his head. "Back."

I took a seat in the small of his back, leaning over to run my tongue all over it. He had a broad back and it took me a while to cover it.

"One last area, Brand." I knew he was referring to his ass. "I want you to lick my ass cheeks and then my crack," he said, firmly.

This was a rare pleasure for me in the world of servicing NOMARs. Usually they did not want you to touch or mess with their asses, for fear they might like it or be thought of as a marked man.

Master had a big furry butt that I enjoyed licking. His smell was musky but not unpleasant, and when I used my hands to separate his butt cheeks, I was rewarded with the sight of his pretty puckered hole, so small, so perfect. I put my tongue to work, licking from the bottom of his crack to the top, purposefully skipping the hole, saving it for last.

Chase bucked and writhed under me, not being used to the sensations I was creating. He jerked wildly when I licked across his hole, causing me to hold onto him for stability. I continued to lick his rosebud, trying to use my teeth to nibble at it.

I pulled up and spit as much of a loogie onto it as I could muster, before going back down and licking it up. With wild abandon, I stuck my tongue into his pink hole, separating his anal ring. I held onto his hips for dear life, because he almost jumped off of the bed. His reaction was common the first time, and I did not let it stop me from exploring his hole with the tip of my tongue before he jerked away from me.

He chuckled with a look of incredulity on his face as he turned towards me. "Ten!" he exclaimed.

I laughed, "But didn't it feel good, Master?"

"I'm not discussing it!" His voice was light-hearted and I knew that he was happy with me. "Now, it's time for your punishment, Brand."

"Yes, sir." I was so excited that I could barely contain myself.

"Lie down."

I put my face into the mattress. "Flip over." I flipped over and watched as Chase went to the other side of the room and picked up a gym bag. I was curious as hell to know what it contained, but knew better than to ask.

He dropped it on the bed and unzipped it. "You are very bad at following directions, Brand. But I'm going to help you get better."

I felt my eyes widen and my pulse quicken. *What the fuck is he going to do?* I got my answer when he pulled a blindfold out of the bag and headed towards me. He had something else in his other hand, but I couldn't see what it was. Master sat down on the mattress beside my head, and I saw that he had his cell phone in his hand. He hit the screen with a big thumb and then placed his phone down on my chest. I glanced down to see that it was on stopwatch mode.

Master gently raised my head and slipped the blindfold onto my face. Everything went dark, and I suddenly became very aware of my breathing and the small sounds in the room.

Chase was right above my face when he spoke next, scaring me a little. "You will receive one torture for every command that you disobeyed."

"I didn't disobey them, Master. I just get carried away with you and your . . ." I clawed to clear my name.

"My what?" he demanded.

"Your body, Master." I felt the heat bloom on my face and neck.

"I enjoy you getting carried away, but it is my job, as your Master, to train you. And I take my job very seriously."

"Yes, Master. I'm sorry, sir."

"No need to apologize, Brand. I find myself drawn to you even more for it. Now, take a drink of water. You're gonna need it." I felt a plastic bottle on my bottom lip and opened my lips to it. Chase gently poured the water into my mouth as he held my head up. I heard a small beep and felt the vibration of his cell phone on my chest.

As soon as I swallowed several gulps of water, the bottle was removed, and a ball gag was immediately put in its place. The ball stretched my mouth open, and I felt Master buckle it around my head. My mind immediately started to race. Ten! Chase had counted to ten when I was licking his whole body. How in the world would I be able to endure ten tortures? I put together in my head that he was timing this, giving me something every few minutes. I hoped that the blindfold and the gag were two of the tortures and that I only had eight more to go.

The minutes passed very slowly. Master touched me every once in a while on different parts of my body. My skin was highly attuned to his touch, and it felt like all the hairs on my body were standing on end when he touched me. The time between the gag and the next event was long. I was hoping for a minute, but it seemed more like ten.

My cock was painfully hard, and I whined for relief.

"Silence." Chase's voice was kind but firm and I stopped whining immediately.

I heard a clicking sound and then the beep and vibration from Master's cell phone. The next torture was a personal favorite of mine. Chase put tit clamps on my nipples in unison, causing me to arch my back and groan.

"That's my boy," Master whispered into my ear.

The pain from the clamps was severe at first. But as the minutes wore on, I either managed the pain better or it subsided more. The constant squeeze on my nipples did nothing for my rock-hard cock except make it hurt even more. I needed relief and I needed it now. I tried to roll over and rub my cock on the comforter, but Master stopped me.

"I didn't tell you to move, Servant." His lips were at my ear again, and his breath warmed my skin. This was the first time that he had referred to me as his Servant, and my heart filled with his words.

I lay still and waited. The waiting was the worst part of all . . .and not being able to see Chase McIntyre . . .and to not be able to talk to him . . .and to not have him inside of me. I was tormented and suddenly realized that was exactly his plan. The cell phone *beep* brought me out of my head.

Torture number four was a ball stretcher, and it felt like Master was trying to pull my balls off. The rubber cuff that he added to the top of my ball sack pulled my balls down to the bottom of my scrotum and stretched out the sack, like an aboriginal woman's neck. Chase made sure not to touch my cock, even though I tried to move it against him while he was working on my balls.

Now I was regretting pushing Master's boundaries while I was following his commands. Why couldn't I have stopped at five or four? But, no! I had to go for ten indiscretions. The cell beeped and I waited for torture number five.

Master's voice was in my ear, "Stand, Brand, and get into your Service Squat." He helped me off the bed and I dropped down into The Squat. I didn't have anything else to do, so I decided to count to myself. *One one thousand, two one thousand, three one thousand.* I hoped that I could tell how long between each torture—more for my state of mind than for anything else.

The burning in my legs surpassed the pain of my balls or my nipples, which was saying something. When I heard the phone beep, I had counted a little over five minutes. It felt so much longer than that.

"Don't move," Master warned me. Torture number six started as a pleasure, but soon turned torturous. Master must have had a feather, and he began to tickle my ass with it. It felt really good at first, but then I wanted to scratch. Knowing that I couldn't scratch that itch on my ass was the true torture of this one. It was the longest five minutes, so far . . .

The next torture came instantly with the beep. With a loud smack, Master spanked me on the ass, driving me forward. Chase's big arm caught me as I lurched forward and righted me again. I waited for the next smack, but instead I got the feather again. It was quickly followed by the paddle again. Master varied the timing of each, so that I never could have guessed when the spank was coming. Soon my ass felt like it was on fire.

Torture number eight involved some rattling and then a terrible pain on my cock. I thought at first that he had set me on fire and I screamed around the ball gag. Once my heart stopped beating so hard, I realized that instead of flames it was ice. The ice burned on my hot cock just like fire, but it did nothing to cool it off. On top of everything else, Master used the feather and the paddle in between touching my cock with the ice.

It had been more than forty minutes since I started to get punished, by my calculations. I had spent over an hour licking and sucking Master before the punishment even began, so I had been sporting this raging hard-on for longer than I even thought was possible. My ass was on fire, matching my nipples and my cock now.

The cell beep was the most welcome sound that I had ever heard when it happened. Master's voice was back in my ear.

"On all fours on the bed, and don't touch your cock." I took my time finding the bed and crawling onto it. I figured that whatever punishment number nine was, I could cut into the time that it was to last.

Master spread my legs apart once I was in position, and then I felt a cool drop of liquid fall onto the top of my ass. That drop ran down my ass crack and onto my puckered hole. Another drop of lube fell on me and dripped down. Just for an added twist, Master had chosen a warming brand of lube that started a slow burn everywhere the lube went. While this slow dripping was annoying, it gave me hope that I was going to get fucked soon, and that thought sustained me. The lube was starting to run down my balls and my legs, making all of the hairs and skin come alive in its path.

Torture number ten was the worst of all. When Master heard the beep of his phone, he crawled onto the bed and into the saddle behind me. I was so elated that the time was here and I was finally going to be full of him. Unfortunately for me, Master had other plans. I felt his big hard cock in the crack of my ass. He placed it in there like a hotdog in a bun and stroked it back and forth. I so badly wanted him to push it into my tight little hole, but he seemed to have no intentions of going in that direction.

Chase continued to friction-fuck my ass, and I wondered if he was going to be able to hold out the whole five minutes. I noticed that as the time went by, Master got faster and more erratic with his rubbing. I needed this to be over now!

When Chase's cell phone beeped for the final time, I almost shot my load right there. I should have been exhausted, but instead I was in the most heightened, sexually aroused state that I had ever been.

"Very nice, Brand. You have pleased me unlike any other marked guy I have been with." Master's voice was heady with need, and I could feel his cock throwing off heat and throbbing like crazy. He reached up and unsnapped the ball gag, freeing my mouth.

I sucked in air in large gulps.

Chase asked, "Are you ready to come, Brand?"

"Yes, Master!" I said excitedly, my voice sounding harsh and unusual.

Chase placed his cock head on my tortured hole and said, "I want you to touch yourself and come on my count. Three, two, one . . ." I barely touched my painfully hard dick and I was already falling into my climax. I came at the very instant that Master got to *one,* and simultaneously, he plowed his throbbing hot poker inside me.

Screaming at the top of my lungs, I felt Master grab hold of my hips and completely bury himself inside of me. My back arched and I threw back my head in complete pleasure and complete pain. I pumped strand after strand of steaming cum onto the bed, shaking from the effort. I had never experienced anything like this before. Master was dominating me like no one ever had — physically, mentally, and completely.

Chase came quickly, as well. He pulled back and only thrust into me once or twice before busting his nut deep inside me. He roared through his climax, sounding like a lion claiming his prey.

"Oh, my fucking God!" he exclaimed.

I was too out-of-breath to say anything.

"Mind if I continue, Brand?"

"I would hurt you if you didn't, Master," I said huskily, hanging my head and feeling his cock start to harden again.

Chase laughed and started to fuck my ass hard and deep. He switched to holding himself still and then moving my hips back and forth, causing me to impale myself over and over on his massive meat-pop. Master was almost there again when he lunged forward, knocking me flat to the mattress.

"Oh, fuck, Master," I moaned into the comforter.

Chase responded by putting his big sweaty palms flat on my shoulder blades and wrapping his legs around mine. His crotch was bearing down on top of mine, and he bounced us on that mattress, causing his cock to drill into me like an oil derrick. It felt like I was being fucked on a trampoline by a huge man with a huge cock . . . and essentially I was!

Master put on a display of fucking like I had rarely felt before. He pounded my ass like he had just been released from a cage himself. I found myself in complete disbelief again that this was now my life. It had been less than two weeks, but it felt like home to me . . . lying under this man . . . being completely filled by him . . . being able to think of nothing but him . . . and knowing that tomorrow would be just the same as today.

CHAPTER FIFTEEN

I woke the next morning in a completely groggy state. I rolled over and cringed. My ass was on fire, and it felt like I could feel every thrust Master had made last night. Not only was my ass feeling it, but the rest of my muscles were sore as hell, and my head felt like it was being played like a drum.

I was alone in the bed. My first thought was that Chase had awoken and didn't wake me, causing me to feel slighted in some way. Good Lord! How in the hell could I feel slighted by him when he gave me his undivided attention for over four hours last night? I was chastising myself when I heard the door open.

"Master," I sighed as I saw him enter. He had two travel mugs of coffee with him.

"You're up," he said, handing me one of the mugs.

"I was just regretting not being able to wake you up properly, Master."

"Jesus! After all that last night and you are still hungry for more . . ."

I was hurt by his words, but more by the sharp pang of realizing that his fascination with me might be over. "You aren't, Master?" If that was the case, my whole world was going to fold in on itself.

Chase put a big hand on my bare shoulder and looked me in the eyes. "You know I am."

Does he mean it?

"I wanted to wake you up a few minutes ago before I got coffee, by fucking you again. But I had you up until five

119

o'clock this morning, so I didn't."

"Really, Master?"

"I don't know what it is about you, but no matter how much we fuck around, I still can't get enough of you." His light-grey eyes stared into mine. His face was nothing but seriousness. "Is it possible that the more I screw your little hole, the tighter it becomes?"

I laughed, and he cracked up with me. Chase McIntyre was my man, and he liked me. It was the best moment of my life. I thought nothing could top the feeling of him being inside me, but I was wrong. Having him tell me that he couldn't get enough of me was like hearing angels sing.

"Come on, let's go shower. Taylor wants to meet with us before dinner."

"Before dinner? What time is it?" I said in shock.

"Three."

"Three o'clock?" Jesus . . . we had slept through the morning and afternoon. "What does Master want to see us for?"

"I don't know, but he sounded all serious," he told me with a shrug of his handsome shoulders.

"Serious? Have I done something wrong?" I felt my stomach drop.

"You haven't done anything wrong, Brand." He pulled me out of the bed and shoved me towards the shower. "If anything, I think I might be the one in trouble," he said quietly as he stepped into the shower.

I followed him in and said, "You?" I lowered my head and looked through my brows at him. "What have you done, Master?"

"Shampoo me," he commanded, turning his back to me.

I jumped to obey. He was able to snap into Master-mode faster than anyone I had ever met before. "Yes, sir." I poured the shampoo into my hand and slowly started to massage it into his scalp. I loved doing these small intimate things to and for my Master.

"Don't make me punish you again." His voice laced the threat with lusty passion, but I couldn't see his face to see if he was mad or not.

I took a chance and quietly asked, "But what if I need to be punished again, Master?"

"I will tell you when you need to be punished, Brand. No one knows that except for me." There was no hint of sarcasm in his voice.

"Yes, sir."

He turned around, putting his head under the water. "Now yours." Master watched as I shampooed my hair, never looking at anything but my eyes.

"Trade places with me," he commanded. Wrapping his big arms around me, he hugged me to his wet body and turned us around. I backed under the water and washed the soap out of my hair.

"Master?"

"Yes, Brand?" His eyes burnt a hole in me and I felt his hardening cock against my stomach. My own cock was hard as a rock and poking his.

"Do you think you will ever get tired of me?"

He looked thoughtful, "Maybe, but not yet. Why?"

"I just want to know what I am in for . . ." I grabbed a pouf and poured shower gel on it.

"I wouldn't want to hurt you, Brand."

"I realize that you probably will move on, but I would like to know first, so I can prepare myself." I began to scrub Master's huge hairy chest with the pouf, producing a huge amount of lather.

He looked at me quizzically. "What are you worried about?"

"I don't want you to be in trouble with Taylor."

"I'm not in trouble . . ." His voice sounded exasperated. "I think I'm just manipulating your time a little too much, that's all."

"I'm the one who has been manipulating you, Master." I soaped his crotch. "Blame it on me, if you need to."

He looked down at me and firmly said, "I won't and I wouldn't."

I kept quiet, scrubbing his long legs and the tops of his feet. He pulled me to my feet and took the pouf from me. Chase scrubbed me clean, front and back. It was an intimate act for a NOMAR, and it turned me on like almost nothing else.

I sucked him off and then cleaned him up again. He jerked me off while he shot water up my asshole with the shower wand. It was a tremendous feeling and I felt closer to him than ever after our talk in the shower. I snuck into my bedroom and got dressed.

Walking with Chase downstairs, I felt every sore spot in my ass. We saw that the fellas were gathered in the den watching a baseball game on TV. They all greeted us warmly, and then the ribbing started. I kept quiet and let Chase fend off the jabs. Happy to see Marshall Taylor joining in on the jesting, I finally relaxed.

"There's a sandwich platter in the kitchen for lunch if you guys are hungry," Master told us. The snickering started immediately.

"I'll make you one, McIntyre," I called to him as I stood up, before he could say anything.

"Two, please!" he yelled back.

"Yes, sir!" I made several sandwiches, piled another plate with fruit and chips, and grabbed two bottles of water. I carried them back to the coffee table in front of the TV, where Chase and I dug into them. Sitting down, even on the soft sofa, made sparks of pain shoot from my ass to my brain.

Master hit the record button on the DVR and then turned the game off. "All right guys, we have some events coming up that we need to plan for," he announced.

Jeremy, Alex, Braden and I looked at each other anxiously.

Master continued, "This weekend we have an away game in Miami, and Thursday we have the New York Shadow Ball."

"The Shadow Ball, Master?" Alex asked.

"It's a charity event, like a meet and greet."

"With a twist," Chase said, with a smirk.

We all turned towards him, but his mouth now was full of turkey and cheese.

"Wealthy people pay enormous amounts to have sex with famous people's Servants and meet us." Master sighed.

"What's the charity, Master?" I asked. I did not mind letting people fuck me for charity, but it had better be for a good cause and something I believed in.

"It's for wounded soldiers and their families."

I smiled and said, "Cool."

"This is Mac's favorite day of the year, isn't it, Chase?" Master goaded him.

"It is," McIntyre blushed slightly.

Marshall addressed all of us, saying, "Each year, groups of wealthy guys come and bring their Servants. Other wealthy men pay to come, like McIntyre. The Masters offer up their time to meet the party-goers and their Servants to fuck them." He turned to look at Chase and said, "It's a real smorgasbord, isn't it?"

"It's like a huge candy store for adults," Chase said, starting to laugh.

"And you are like the biggest kid in the candy store, Mac," Master teased.

"It's a lot of ass!"

"I think that last year, you tried to fuck every one of them, didn't you?"

"Absolutely!"

We all laughed, but I was immediately jealous. The thought of McIntyre with other guys made me crazy.

Master turned to me and said, "Well, I guess this year you will be hogging Brand over there . . ."

Oh, shit! Here we go!

Chase looked at me and replied, "I'm sure Brand won't mind having a break from me." And then hastily added, "For charity, of course."

We all burst out laughing at that, and he kept the most innocent look on his face.

I took the opportunity to change the subject off of us by asking, "Master, when you have an away game, will you take the four of us?"

"Of course," he answered matter-of-factly. "You will follow the same routine as you did on Sunday."

"Awesome!" One thing that I loved to do was travel, and I had always hoped to see the world when I became a Servant. So far, this whole experience was working out fantastically, but in the back of my mind was that thought of Master wanting to meet with me and Chase.

Marshall went on to tell us what a great job we were doing and how he was proud of us. I felt like he might be one of the nicest Masters ever. And we were the luckiest Servants ever. The waves of positive feelings ended abruptly when he turned the game back on and then asked to see the two of us. I swallowed hard and felt my heart drop into my stomach.

I followed the two NOMARs into a study on the same floor. I had never been in this room before and was immediately distracted by all of the sports memorabilia and framed photographs on the walls. There was a desk with a ton of fan mail on it and boxes of footballs and pictures waiting for his autograph.

"Have a seat, guys." He indicated two black leather armchairs. I sat down gingerly, trying not to sit directly on my ass.

"What's this all about, Marsh?" Chase asked right before

grabbing an apple and crunching into it.

"Something important I wanted to discuss with you."

I could see that now that Master was set to begin, he was having either second thoughts or nerves about how to deliver the message. Telling myself to keep quiet, I willed him to go on.

Chase's loud apple chewing would have been comical if I didn't feel like I would throw up any second. Master looked at him and raised his eyebrows. Chase chewed less noisily.

Marshall looked like he was far away when he finally managed to start. "When I would let you spend the night or whatever with Brand, I thought you guys were just fucking."

"We were . . . are," Chase said with a full mouth.

"I assumed that you were fucking a lot, I mean, I know my man, Mac, here, and I just assumed that he was fucking you raw all those times."

He was . . .

Master grabbed a remote off of his desk and pointed it at a huge screen on the wall. "And then I saw this . . ." The screen blazed to life with a direct shot of Chase's bedroom. He was lying on the bed and I was licking him from toe to head.

I blushed furiously and felt the bile rise into my throat.

"You recorded us?" McIntyre asked in disbelief.

Master turned back to us and said, "I record every room in my house, every day. I usually don't pay much attention to them, but when you guys missed lunch today, I took a quick peek."

I was glad that I wasn't supposed to talk, because I don't know what I would have said.

"I've never seen anything like it." Master's voice wasn't mad or disappointed. If I had to guess his tone, I think it would have been awe.

"And then when the punishment came . . ." Master aimed the remote and held down a button. Chase's deep voice boomed instructions out to me.

"Are you mad at me, Marsh?" Chase asked with all the innocence of a child.

Master turned back to him with a glazed look in his eyes, which he shook off and said, "God, no!" He turned to me and said, "It was the hottest thing I had ever seen. I beat off twice, watching it."

We all laughed, and then Chase said, "So, you're not mad?"

"No. I wanted to know from you, Mac, if this is what I'm supposed to be doing for my Servants."

Chase looked over at me and shrugged, "I guess."

"Is this how a Master is supposed to be?"

"I enjoy it, Marsh. And you know I do what I enjoy . . ." He chuckled.

Master turned to me and said, "Brand, is that what I should be doing?"

I was at a loss for words, but eventually found them. "Master, I think you are one of the most amazing, kindest, cutest men that there are in this world and the four of us love you, just as you are."

"Thanks. I thought I knew what I was doing until I saw this." He indicated the screen.

"That's different, Master," I said quietly.

"I know it's different! I have never seen two people fuck like you two did when you were finished with the punishments. But what do you mean when you say it's different?"

Before I could answer, Chase spoke. "Marsh, I don't know how to explain it, but I'm drawn to Brand and he to me. I've never experienced anything like his ass before, but I think that's only part of it."

"Oh?" Master asked.

McIntyre looked afraid suddenly, and I was left wondering what he was going to say.

"You know me, Marsh, I've had a lot of sex . . ."

"That's an understatement!" Master laughed and then turned to me and said, "No offense, Brand."

"None taken, Master."

"I'm serious." Chase scoffed. He lowered his voice and said, "I've fucked a lot of tail, and there was something that happened last night that I've never experienced." He shyly and quickly glanced at me, causing the blood to rush to my dick.

I expected Master to say something like, "Really?", but instead he said, "I know."

Chase and I jerked our heads towards him.

Marshall Taylor pointed the remote at the screen and fast forwarded to the point where I came at the exact second that Chase plowed into my sore ass. "When I saw this, I knew that it was something different. I knew that you two had something also."

"What?" I blurted out before I could even stop myself.

They both turned towards me.

"Sorry, Master."

"So, I thought you guys were just banging it out, but when I saw that . . ." He pointed at the screen. "I knew that I needed to . . . to . . . adjust our situation."

"What are you saying, Marshall?" Chase asked, using his best friend's first name in a rare instance.

Master took his time answering, looking from Chase to me slowly. "Mac, I think you are Brand's true Master."

I was shocked as hell.

Apparently, so was Chase McIntyre, because his mouth hung open at his friend. "What?"

"I may not know how to be a great Master, but there is one thing that I know, and that is how a team works best. There is no question in my mind that you and Brand are a team that works well together. I also have no doubt that you should be

Brand's Master."

I couldn't believe that I was hearing my Master say the very thing that I had fantasized that he would say.

"Don't you agree with me, Brand?"

I swallowed hard and agreed with him, "Yes, sir. Nothing against you, Master."

"Of course not. It just happened, I'm sure, and neither of you have control over it." Master's eyes bored into me. "How would you like McIntyre to be your Master, in every way?"

"It would be the most unbelievable thing I could ever dream of, Master." I paused and then added, "If he would have me as his Servant . . ."

Marshall smiled and smirked, "Well, McIntyre?"

Chase leaned back, tented his fingers, and smirked as well, "The things I could do with Brand, if he was mine . . ."

"So that's a yes?" I asked, holding my breath.

"Yes, Brand, I will be your Master," he said pointedly.

Marshall said, "Good. I'm glad that is settled. We can start the paperwork to transfer The Service contract."

"I have a few stipulations first, Master, if I may be so bold."

Both NOMARs whipped their heads at me, McIntyre smirking up a storm. "If I was your Master right now, you would so get punished for that."

"I'm sorry, Masters." I lowered my head, more to hide my smile than to be subservient.

"I'm very interested to hear your demands, Brand," Marshall said, sarcasm dripping from his words.

CHAPTER SIXTEEN

"My demands are simple, Master," I said smiling broadly. Marshall Taylor had just told me that he believed that my true Master was Chase McIntyre and that he was going to start the paperwork to transfer me to him. McIntyre had agreed to become my Master, making me the happiest Servant in the world.

Chase just stared at me with his light-grey eyes blazing, but Master smiled and said, "Hit us with them."

I was loving having both of them focused on me and hanging on my every word. It gave me a rush having these two Masters at my command, so to speak. "Well, first, I really love living here and I think Chase does also." I looked over at Marshall and saw him shake his head in the affirmative. "I love being around you, Master, and my boys, of course."

"And so your demand is . . ."

"If Chase doesn't mind, I would like us to live here with you guys." I immediately blushed, knowing that this was way outside the boundaries of my position.

"I can't wait to punish you for this." McIntyre smirked at me like I was the fly caught in the spider's web.

"Yes, sir." I felt the familiar slow burn begin in my ass and my balls sent an electric shock up my spine, indicating a hard-on was imminent.

"I would love for you guys to live here," Marshall gushed. "Done!"

"My second demand is that the cameras need to be removed from Chase's room, Master."

"You telling me what to do, Brand?" Master smiled and left me wondering what it meant.

"He needs more training, Marsh. I'm on it," Chase said, starting to laugh. "But I agree with him that if we are going to live here, we need some privacy."

"I agree. I'm just playing with you guys. And what's next, Brand?"

"I would like to have a copy of that, Master." I pointed at the screen and blushed furiously. The scene on the screen was Chase drilling me for the second time without even pulling out of me. I remembered every moment of it — the smell, the feel, the power he had over me, the taste of him, and mostly the realization on my part that he was mine and I belonged to him.

"Want to watch that again, do you, Brand?" Master asked, lasciviously.

"Yes, sir."

"Who wouldn't? It was the single most awesome sex I have ever had," Chase said without hesitation, his eyes burrowing a hole in me.

"High praise from Mac!" His best friend laughed.

I decided to stay quiet, for a change.

"I think I can certainly meet your demands, Brand. And I have one of my own."

Both of our heads turned towards him in surprise.

"I will hear your demand now, Master," I said smugly.

"Oh, you are asking for it, Mister," McIntyre growled.

Marshall laughed and said, "Well, you know Mac and I have been good friends for a long time."

I shook my head.

"And there is something I have always wanted to do, but have not had the opportunity."

What could that be?

He took a deep breath and said, "I've always wanted to fuck a guy with Mac."

"We've done that, Marsh," Chase said, looking confused.

"No, I would like us to DP Brand."

Double penetrate! Holy fuck! Both of those guys had huge cocks and I couldn't even imagine them inside my little ass at the same time.

McIntyre was immediately on the defensive. "Man, we are both so big. It might really hurt Brand."

"It might, but with his ability to tighten up right after, he might just be the only one we could ever do it with. What do you think, Brand?"

"I'm willing to give it a shot, Master, since you are doing this extraordinary thing for Chase and me. I would, of course, have a few conditions . . ."

McIntyre immediately smirked and said, "Enough!" I could tell that he was secretly enjoying me being out of line.

"Mac, you willing to give it a try for me?" Marshall checked with his best friend.

"Who could say no to that?" he asked, throwing his hands up in acceptance.

"Good. We will wait until we hear back from The Service about the transfer before we hear Brand's conditions. Now, let's go take the boys to play some golf. How about it?"

"Sounds fun, Master." The way my ass was burning, I knew that it was going to be painful to walk and play golf today, but I refused to be left out or show any signs of weakness.

Taylor addressed McIntyre, saying, "I'm going to invite Austin and Quinn to go with us so we will have two foursomes."

"Master, can I go tell the guys the news now?"

"Yes."

"Thank you, Master." I cautiously got out of the chair, noticing that Chase was watching me carefully, and quickly left the room. Rejoining the boys in front of the TV, I plopped down on a pillow with a huge smile on my face.

Jeremy immediately muted the TV and said, "What was that all about?"

Alex and Braden leaned in to hear every word. "Master has this whole house recorded," I whispered. They all had a look of *Oh, shit!* on their faces. "He said that when McIntyre and I missed lunch, he was concerned, so he watched the feed in our room."

"What the fuck were you two doing?" Alex asked.

"We were having four hours of the most amazing sex that I have ever had!" I blurted out, laughing and snorting.

"Four hours?" Jeremy asked in awe.

"It was incredible, fellas."

"Was Master mad?" Alex asked.

"Not at all. Master apparently felt it was like nothing he had ever seen before as well, and he decided on the spot that McIntyre was my true Master."

"What?" the normally quiet Braden asked in disbelief.

"No fucking way!" Jeremy spat.

"That's what I thought also. It was the last thing I ever would have expected."

"Wow."

"I was stunned." The three of them sat in silence, chewing over this information.

"So, what happens next?" Braden asked.

"He asked me what I thought."

"And?"

I rolled my eyes at them, "You guys know how I feel about McIntyre, and you certainly can see how he feels about me."

"Yeah, we know . . ." Jeremy sighed.

I continued, "So, he asked Chase and he was all for it. Master is going to contact The Service and ask for a transfer of the contract!"

The guys all jumped up and congratulated me by hugging and high-fiving. When they had settled down and were seated again, I told them about my three demands. They were laughing hysterically at my story and commenting on my huge brass balls when my two Masters walked into the room.

"What's this about brass balls?" Master asked with a smile.

"We were just saying that Brand has huge ones, Master," Jeremy said quickly.

"That he does," Master agreed.

"Yeah, well, we're gonna be polishing the brass tonight," Chase promised, drawing a chorus of sounds from the other guys and making me blush under his gaze.

Marshall addressed us saying, "How would you guys like to play a little golf today?"

I saw the panicked look cross Alex and Braden's faces as they listened. I guessed that they didn't play golf.

He continued, "I'm going to invite two of my buddies, and we will have two foursomes."

"What if we have never played before, Master?" Alex asked.

"Who doesn't play?"

"I don't," Alex answered.

"Me either," Braden added.

Jeremy and I nodded our heads, indicating that we played.

"Well, the two best players are Mac and I, so you two can go with us, and we will show you what to do."

I was surprised that I was going to be separated from Chase, but I figured it wouldn't be the last time. If I was being truly honest about it, my first reaction was to be jealous. I didn't want to think about Alex and Braden satisfying my new Master, but I knew I could deal with it.

On the way upstairs to change into golfing attire, Chase pulled me into his room and said, "Is this what you really want, Brand?"

"What? To be separated from you for golf?" I asked, dismayed.

"No. Do you want to really be my Servant like you said?"

My heart melted at his sincerity. "Yes, Master. You are my true Master, and I want more than anything to belong to you."

He grinned from ear to ear and smirked. "Good!" Then his brow creased and he asked, "Are you concerned about golf?"

"Not really, Master. I mean, we will be together tonight, right?"

"Absolutely, if it is all right with Marsh."

I smiled and said, "Cool." I turned towards the door, needing to still get dressed for our golf game.

Chase grabbed my arm and added, "The guys that Marsh is inviting are nice. I want you to entertain them, if they want to . . . which they will."

"If that is what you desire, Master," I said, raising an eyebrow.

"What I desire is to punish you right now, but we have to get going," he said with a smirk.

"Damn golf game." I smirked back.

"You are so gonna pay . . ."

"And dearly, I hope." I laughed as I broke from his laserlike gaze and headed to my room.

CHAPTER SEVENTEEN

A ustin and Quinn joined us at the country club. My two Masters were members of the club, which was super fancy and exclusive. We were gathered in the bar, having a drink, when they walked in. Our group was already garnering a lot of attention. I don't think most men had seen a group of four Servants together in one place, ever.

Austin was short and thick. He had huge biceps for someone his size, and I was delighted to see that he had tattoos on the backs of them. His brown hair was buzz-cut into a skullcap. He had a nice face with an easy smile, blond soul-patch on his chin under his bottom lip, and a heavy shadow of a beard that framed his square jaw perfectly.

Quinn didn't look like Austin at all. He had black hair that stuck out of his white baseball cap, which he wore backwards. He was tall with an average frame. His face was handsome with a thick black goatee, but no mustache. He looked like a good-natured guy who had a smirk on his face, reminding me of Chase.

Chase and Marshall greeted the two friends warmly and then introduced them to each of us. Quinn showed no emotion on his face as he shook our hands, but Austin visibly leered, licking his lips and constantly readjusting his junk. I found him much easier to read than Quinn and knew exactly how I could use my body to manipulate him. Marshall pointed at Jeremy and me, saying that we were going to accompany the two of them today.

"Fuck me! I won't be able to concentrate on my play!"

Austin exploded.

"Well then, let's just make a little bet on the play then, shall we?" Marshall challenged him.

"What's the bet?" Quinn asked quietly.

McIntyre spoke up and said, "If you win, you get an hour with your two partners there."

"And if you win?" Austin asked.

"You will have to beat off while Marsh and I have fun with all four of them!"

"That's bullshit!" Austin spit.

"Scared?" Marshall chided.

"Marsh, we just thought we could play today and then . . . you know . . . have a little party afterwards," Austin said, suddenly frustrated.

"And you still might," McIntyre said pointedly.

"If you perform . . ." Marshall added.

"We're in," Quinn said confidently.

"Quinn!" Austin yelled.

"What? We have a chance to fuck with these four Servants, who are experts in pleasing NOMARs! I'm taking the chance!" He was so excited that he actually broke into a smile.

"Fuck!" Austin had to admit that Quinn was right. Turning towards Taylor and McIntyre, he conceded, saying, "Okay. Let's do this thing."

"Awesome! We can play four-ball, closest to the hole," Marshall announced.

We moved from the bar to the locker room, receiving numerous stares on our way. I was proud to be with my two famous Masters and held my head up high in the hallway and the locker room. Chase gave me a *good luck* squeeze of my ass before we left the locker room and told me that I'd better play up to my best or I would have to answer to him for it.

Chase, Marshall, Alex and Braden went off first. Master had arranged four carts for us with sets of clubs. The two

NOMARs spent a while showing Alex and Braden what to do to use a driver, and it was almost comical. Several times as I watched, I wished it was me with Chase, who had his big body wrapped around Alex showing him how to swing or stand.

The lessons were soon over and they were teeing off. Master hit a fantastic shot, and I tried not to laugh at Alex and Braden's worm-burners. Chase looked like a dark God in his stance, every muscle attuned to the one purpose of hitting a small white ball off of a small white tee. His swing was beautiful, but his muscled form kept him from being as graceful as he needed to be. Regardless, his shot was long and straight. I felt proud that he was going to be my Master and that this big strong athlete wanted me.

"Take that!" Chase said to us as they piled in their golf carts and moved up the green. I watched as they located and picked up the balls of Alex, Braden and McIntyre and then the four of them shot at the green from where Master's ball was lying. Soon they were clear of the fairway, and my group took some practice swings before driving.

I was nervous to hit in front of everyone, but I drove it pretty long and to the left. Jeremy also hit well, as did, Austin. Quiet Quinn had the best shot, finishing slightly behind the spot Master had hit to. The four of us played well. Quinn was obviously the best driver, and the other three of us were excellent putters and had decent short games.

The lead group texted their score after each hole, so we knew that we were tied going into hole number three. We lost that hole and now were down one. We were able to tie it up three holes later and finished the front nine tied. The eight of us descended on the clubhouse bar, talking about our good shots and the ones that got away from us.

Chase pulled me to the side and asked, "You're playing your best, Brand?"

"Of course, Master," I smiled at him. "I can't bring myself to lose. I'm too competitive."

"That's my boy!" he said as he smacked me on the ass. I left him feeling all warm inside from his words, and my crotch had that familiar twinge in it that signaled my arousal.

"Nine holes for the victory, fellas!" Marshall shouted as he led us out of the bar and onto the tenth hole tee-box.

Austin hit an amazing shot from the sand-trap on number ten and we went up by a point. Trash-talking seemed to be my team's specialty, so we really rubbed it in, especially because they were not able to tie it up again until the seventeenth hole. We all watched as Master's group teed off. Alex and Braden had improved immensely since the beginning, but I could tell that they were exhausted from the effort.

Quinn hit a tremendous drive off the tee-box for our group, and Austin's approach had us on the green in two. We knew that the other group had made a par-4, so we had two chances to tie it up. Our ball was on the green, but it was really far from the hole . . . a good 30 feet away.

Jeremy putted first since he had been the hottest with the putter. He misread the slope and didn't even come close. Austin went next and got much closer, but still a good five feet away. Quinn had been studying the others' lines and ran his right by the hole, not having the speed correct. Now, it was all up to me.

Marshall, Chase, Alex, and Braden were all standing on the edge of the green watching. I pulled my putter out of my bag and walked all around the green, trying desperately to see the different contours of it. When I got closer to the watching group, I could hear their little snide remarks as they tried to get into my head.

Chase motioned me over. He pulled me into a headlock with a muscled arm and whispered to me, "You put that ball in that hole, young one."

"Will I get punished if I don't, Master?" I whispered back.

"You will get punished if you do, Brand," he stated matter-of-factly. His voice was heavy with lust and need. "If you don't, I will be so disappointed."

Austin came over, yelling, "Hey, get off our player! You can't intimidate him!"

If Austin only knew the truth. No one intimidated and motivated me like Chase McIntyre. I would do anything to not disappoint him and personally, I didn't want to miss a punishment session with my new Master at any cost. What was curious to me was the fact that Chase wanted me to play so well when I was opposing him. That part I did not understand, but my job was to follow his commands, always.

Austin joined my other teammates and told me, "You can do this. Hit it just like Quinn did, but not as hard."

Nodding my head in agreement, I walked back to the ball and took up my stance over it. I took a quick peek at McIntyre and I saw him subtly ball his fist and shake it slightly down and back up, as if to say, *Do it!*

Exhaling hard, I pulled the putter back and let it swing like a pendulum. The putter struck the ball firmly and I watched as it took off, rolling over the rises and scooting down the valleys. The little white ball looked like it was on a good line and it headed directly for the hole. Then I realized that it was slowing down.

"Go, go, go!" I willed it to continue, but I could see that it was going to stop right before the hole. The ball stopped rotating right in front of the hole. I couldn't see the hole, so I didn't know how close it was. Starting to walk towards the hole, I was amazed when the ball fell in. My team went bonkers in front of me and I turned to see Chase's smirk and his raised fist. Master's group, minus Chase, hung their heads while clapping at my shot.

Jeremy, Austin, Quinn and I high-fived and shouted out

our enthusiasm. We walked over to the first group and shook hands. McIntyre grabbed my hand and pulled me into a bear hug, saying loud enough for everyone to hear, "Oh, Brand, you are going to pay for that last shot!" In my ear, he whispered, "I'm very proud of you, young one."

"Thanks, Master," I whispered back. My cock was rockhard, responding to his touch, his pride, his excitement, and his words.

We piled in the golf carts and headed to the clubhouse. When we parked, Marshall told someone from the club that we were in need of a private room. I was still very much on a high from hitting the winning shot, but I realized that shortly I was going to be entertaining Master's friends and probably Chase would be sampling Alex or Braden, or both, for the very first time. I felt helpless to do anything about it, and had to tell myself that he would come back to me afterwards.

We were shown to a private room that had a fully stocked bar, several big couches, flat screen TVs, and expensive looking end-tables. The club employee backed out, closing the door behind him. Austin had already descended on the bar and had begun to make a pitcher of drinks.

My fellow Servants and I excused ourselves to go use the restroom before the fun started. We gossiped quickly about what was about to happen, each one of us trying to make ourselves as presentable as possible. On our way back into the room, I saw Chase down the hall on his cell phone. As we approached him, he reached out, grabbed my arm, and pulled me to the side. Putting away his phone, he watched until the other three Servants disappeared into the room.

Held between the wall and his big body, I felt closer to him than ever. He turned his husky gaze on me and commanded, "Open."

I immediately opened my mouth and he spit a big loogie into it.

"You are mine. I keep your mouth and your ass full of my cum, and you belong to me." He could not have spelled it out any plainer for me. I was absolutely enthralled with him and would do whatever he wanted me to do, no matter what it was.

"Yes, Master." My voice was pure breathy awe.

"You will do as I command you to."

"Yes, sir. Of course, Master."

"I want you to let Quinn and Austin fuck you."

"Yes, sir."

"And when they are done, I want you to put the tip of your finger onto Austin's puckered hole and then push it in." I looked at Chase in shock. A marked man could get killed doing that to a NOMAR. "He will get turned on, and then he will want you to fuck him."

"Master?" I was in disbelief of what he was telling me. It was rare for a NOMAR to like to get fucked, and even if Austin was one of those people, I couldn't believe he would want to get fucked in front of his friends.

"Do as I say."

"Yes, sir."

"And Brand . . ."

"Yes, sir?"

"When you fuck him, I want it to be with the same intensity and power that you showed before the game Sunday. Do you remember?"

I smiled broadly, saying, "Yes, sir."

"Don't disappoint me."

"No, sir." It was the absolute last thing I would want to do. He let me go and we quickly walked back into the private room.

"There you are!" Austin shouted. He was completely naked and waiting like a petulant child. Jeremy had his face planted in Quinn's crotch, sucking with all of his might.

"Chill out, Austin," Chase yelled back. "And remember that Brand's the one that won it for you."

I could tell by his face that Austin had not considered this before. I smirked to my future Master as I undressed. I soon had my mouth wrapped around Austin's nice-sized cock. He was a short man, so the average-sized dick looked extremely big on him. He tasted fresh, and I slobbed his knob with all my skills.

Hearing a noise to the side, I cut my eyes over to see that Quinn was walking towards me, his cock poking into his stomach. Austin was already hard, so when he pulled his dick out of my mouth, he immediately went over and fed it into Jeremy's ass from behind. I sucked Quinn into my mouth, slicking him up. Quinn pulled it out of me and then slapped me across the face with it before he lowered himself down to the floor.

Quinn sat down and held his cock up for me. I lubed him and then straddled his legs. He placed his small cock head against my rosebud, grabbed both of my hip bones, and pulled me down onto his length. Placing my hands flat on his chest, I got into a rhythm of riding him up and down. I enjoyed that his cock punched my prostate repeatedly as he worked me up and down his pole.

Looking around me, I saw that Austin was giving Jeremy quite the fucking on one side of me, and Alex and Braden were naked and sucking on my two Master's cocks on the other side. Even though Chase's dick was being blown, his gaze was laser-locked onto mine. Responding to his stare, I bore down on Quinn and finished him off. He held me down on his pole and shot strands of hot cum all over the inside of my ass.

"Fuck me," Quinn said, in a moment of exuberance. "This one is fantastic!" he yelled at Austin.

Austin was just finishing inside Jeremy, collapsing on top

of him and howling. I continued to ride Quinn's sensitive pole up and down as I watched Alex try to sit in Chase's lap. Chase's cock was huge, and none of these Servants were quite ready for it.

"Let's switch places!" Austin called out to Quinn. I stood up and saw that Braden was impaled on Marshall's cock and they were both watching the show.

Austin motioned for me to clean up his sloppy cock and suck him back up hard again, so I did. His cum tasted nutty and sweet, like pecan pie a little bit. It didn't take him long to get hard again, and soon he had me bent in half on my back. I noticed that Quinn was taking a little more time to fuck the second time and that Alex could only get about three-quarters of Chase's huge pole inside him before he had to stop. Both of these things made me smile to myself as Austin mounted me and began to give me a good fucking.

Austin was energetic, that was for sure. He pounded my sweet pud repeatedly, mumbling about how tight I was, how lucky Marshall was, and how fortunate he was to be friends with him.

I was getting a little nervous about my assignment from Chase as the time approached rapidly. He fortified my nerves with his eyes each and every time that I looked over at him. Even though his big fat cock was buried inside someone else's hot ass, he was totally commanding me from long distance.

Austin had just reached his second climax, yelling, "I'm fucking coming up in that sweet little ass!" He threw back his head and closed his eyes as his hips continued to thrust his cock into me through the sensitivity of his climax.

I took my chance, leaning up, and swooping my hand behind his ass. My fingertips found his tight little asshole and I watched as his eyes flew open. Not wanting to waste my opportunity, I shoved my hand forward and buried two of my fingers inside him.

I thought that Austin would be mad and maybe even hit me, but instead he moaned quietly and arched his back. He came back to himself, looking shamefully over at Chase and Marshall. They appeared to be busy fucking Alex and Braden, even though I knew they were both watching Austin and trying not to laugh.

Austin looked back at me and said, "You wanna feel what it's like to fuck a NOMAR, Servant boy?"

"Yes, sir," I answered excitedly.

"Well, let's see what you can do," Austin said, pulling out of me and getting down on all fours. I grabbed the bottle of lube, smirking at my Masters while Austin couldn't see.

"Austin, you exhausted?" Marshall yelled.

"Something like that," he grumbled.

I jacked my cock and then slammed it into Austin's tight little hole. He bit his lip and howled in pain as his anal ring flew apart and I slid into him. The whole room had stopped what they were doing and were watching us. I gave Austin a fucking that he would not soon forget. When I came inside him, I roared with my climax and slammed as far inside him as I could get.

Pulling my still-shooting cock out of his ass, I milked more cum onto his puckered hole and then pushed myself back into his now even tighter hole. "Breeding that fucking NOMAR ass," I said as I slapped his ass, causing everyone in the room to burst out laughing.

"That's my fucking boy," I heard Chase McIntyre say as I finally pulled out of Austin and helped him to his feet.

"Not yet, he's not," Marshall yelled back. "He's still my boy while he's fucking like that!"

"Nice ass, Austin," I told him as I helped him stand.

"Where did you learn to do that?" Austin asked, awe in his quiet voice and a small tremor in his legs.

"Mac," I said with a chuckle. "As hard as I just fucked you, he drills me that hard or harder every single day." I returned the tone of his soft voice, not letting the others hear.

"Fuck!"

"Exactly!" I laughed, heading over to my two Masters.

CHAPTER EIGHTEEN

M arshall told Chase that he could have me again for the night and showed us where to disconnect the cameras. I could barely contain myself waiting to be with him. It was obvious he was proud as a peacock for both of my performances today, and I was so ready to be rewarded or punished, since they were the same thing in my book.

"Go to our room," Chase commanded me. I was so excited to hear him refer to that bedroom as ours that I almost ran. He kept me waiting for quite some time before he finally joined me.

"On the bed, and get those clothes off," he demanded, seemingly ignoring me as he headed to the bathroom.

When he emerged from the bathroom, he was completely naked and looking like a great muscular man sandwich, which I couldn't wait to eat. His big cock was already hard and bouncing out from his crotch, framed by his dark pubic hair. I wanted that monster inside me right at that moment.

Chase circled around the bed like he was a great white shark and the bed was a raft holding his lunch. His light-grey eyes took in the whole scene and kept me firmly rooted to the bed. Finally he stopped walking and pushed my torso down onto the mattress.

"I'm going to satisfy myself on different parts of your body tonight. Do you understand, Servant?"

"Yes, Master." My voice was breathy and fraught with tension.

His smirk was back as he said, "I'm doing this as your

punishment for beating me today at golf. Do you understand?"

"Yes, Master."

"Even though you beat me today, you performed exceptionally, and for that there will probably be some small reward . . . later."

"Yes, sir!" I perked up.

"And you also performed an exceptional feat at the after-party, which I will not soon forget."

"Me either, Master."

"Don't make me gag you, Brand."

I swallowed hard, saying, "Sorry, Master. I guess I have many lessons yet to learn."

"And I will teach you those lessons." His words practically seared a hole in me with their pointedness. "Now, open."

I immediately opened my mouth wide. He hooked my open mouth with an over-sized thumb and pulled my head towards him. Kneeling with one knee on the bed, Chase spit a huge loogie into my mouth and said, "Let me see it."

I closed my mouth slightly and stuck out my tongue, showing him his ball of spit.

"Swallow." He watched me and stroked my throat as I swallowed. "Who do you belong to?"

"You, Master."

"And who keeps you filled up with his sweet juice?"

"You, Master."

"That's right." Chase reached under my armpits and pulled me towards the edge of the bed. I thought he was going to pull me right off of the bed, but he stopped when my head cleared the mattress. It now hung over the edge and he wasted no time in filling my gaping maw with his fat cock.

I sucked his meaty tool with all my might. Sucking cock upside-down was a new experience, and I struggled with the saliva issue for a minute before figuring out that I had to swallow more often. Chase put his hands on my rib cage, leaned over me, and began to fucking drill my mouth. It was all I could do to hold on for the ride. My Master was in total control and dominating me as only he could.

Mac came quickly, producing a tremendous amount of salty, sweet man-cream, which I tried to swallow down as quickly as I could. A huge moan escaped him as he shot strand after strand of his cream into me. He massaged my throat again as I swallowed, finally pulling back while keeping his still dripping cock head on my tongue.

"Show me," he commanded, his breathing still ragged.

I pushed his cum out of my mouth, letting it run down the sides and on top of his shaft.

"Good. Now, swallow it down."

I did.

He asked, "Who's cum do you like the best?"

"Yours, Master."

"That's right." Chase milked his big lap-hog for more cum before withdrawing it from my mouth. He kept the head against my skin, trailing it over my eyes, nose, and forehead. Then I felt it on my ear and down my neck. He tickled my nipple with it, and as it cleared my stomach, I saw that Master was getting hard again from this light touching. His cock head continued all the way down my legs and onto my feet, sending cold chills running up my spine.

With one big hand on my hip, Master turned me so that my head was back on the mattress and my legs were now hanging over the side. He lifted my legs, putting my feet together and said, "Hold."

My future Master walked to the nightstand and grabbed a bottle of lube, taking his sweet time, while I tried to hold my legs in the air in the shape he had made. My leg muscles strained to hold the position, and I felt the tension in my stomach. Walking back towards me, he pushed my feet against his muscled chest, giving me instant relief. Master smirked at me as he squirted lube into his hand.

I was curious as hell what Chase had planned. He surprised me by lubing the bottoms of my feet before lubing his dick up. Putting my feet back together, I knew what the deal was now, so I arched my feet, letting only my heels and toes touch. Master smiled as he saw the hole open between my feet, and he lowered my legs down as he backed away from the bed. When the angle was right, he inserted his cock into the hole created by the bottoms of my feet and begun to fuck into it.

He really is going to relieve himself again while I wait?

My cock was painfully hard against my stomach, and my ass was itching to be fucked. In my head I knew this was my punishment, to have to wait for my pleasure. But in my heart I knew that I would endure this and whatever else my new Master wanted to do to me in order to have his attention, like I was getting in spades at the moment.

McIntyre, to his credit, fucked my feet with all of the seriousness and power that he had just used when face-fucking me. I loved the heat that was being generated by him and loved even more when he fell over the edge of his climax and sprayed hot cum all over my stomach and chest.

"Oh, fuck me." He sighed.

"Exactly what I was thinking, Master," I said quickly, before I could stop myself.

He stopped moving immediately and stared at me. Chase pulled his sloppy cock away from my feet and walked over to the dresser. Removing the ball gag from a drawer, he came back to the bed and strapped it into place on my head. The ball stretched my lips around its rubber form and I tried my best not to make whining noises behind it.

"There. That's better, yes?"

Not being able to speak, I nodded my head in agreement instead.

"Yes, I thought so." Master had also brought a towel with him from the dresser and used it now to clean my torso off. I hated that he was wasting that delicious seed, but I was really in no position to do anything about it.

Now, because of my outburst, Master certainly couldn't give me what I needed yet. He turned me over onto my stomach by putting his big hands on my hip and shoulder and pushing. I tried to turn my head to the side so that I could see what he was up to, but it was uncomfortable with the gag in place, and I settled for a partial turn.

Chase squirted lube into my ass crack, and then I heard him jacking his cock again. On any given normal day, I would completely be in awe of his stamina and sexual prowess, but in this case it worked against me. He could continue to torment me while satisfying himself over and over.

When I felt his weight on the bed, I smiled to myself into the mattress. I loved having his weight on top of me, even if it was just on my backside. He straddled my legs like he was riding a horse, letting his stallion-sized member lay on the crack of my ass.

His deep voice was in my ear, "Are you going to be good if I take the gag off?"

I tried to say I would around the gag while nodding. Chase removed the gag and hooked the corner of my mouth with his thick thumb, pulling it to the side so that he could see part of my face.

"I know you have questions you want to ask me, Brand . . ."

"Yes, sir."

"You may ask."

"You fucked Alex today, Master . . ."

"I tried," he chuckled. "What's your question, Brand?"

I swallowed hard, wishing now that I would not have gone down this path. But I had to know. "Did Master like him better than me?" I blurted it out all at once, making myself sound even more pathetic than I was.

"Are you kidding me?" I could feel Chase's cock respond to our talking. "He was nothing compared to you, Brand."

It was exactly what I wanted him to say, and I felt the heat bloom in my chest, my cheeks, and in my balls. This man was the most perfect person that I had ever met and I was thrilled to be part of his life.

"Is that it? The only question you have is one that you know the answer to already?"

"No. I just wondered how you knew that Austin would re-act the way he did today, Master."

"A friend of a friend told me that he had seen it happen once before, so I thought it might be interesting to see what happened . . ." McIntyre laughed out loud, adding, "And, boy, did you make it happen."

"Did Master enjoy the show?" I smirked.

"You were masterful. But you know that you cannot be the Master here, don't you?"

"Yes, sir."

"Because I am your Master, Brand. Say it!"

"You are my Master, sir."

His voice was deep and husky when he spoke again, "Tell me what you want your Master to do, Brand."

"I want my Master to fuck me, hard and deep. Punish me, Master."

"Your punishment is over, Brand. It's time for me to re-ward you, as only your true Master can."

It was like music to my ears. Grinding my ass cheeks into his crotch, I felt Master harden to his full length against me. My own cock was so painfully hard and being rubbed be-tween me and the comforter as McIntyre started his fuck mo-tion between my buns.

"Master, I'm gonna come!" I groaned.

"Not yet, Brand." His command was like concrete, unable to be broken in my mind. I concentrated on thinking of nothing but a smelly baby's diaper I had seen in the parking lot of the golf course. It didn't make my hard-on decrease at all, but it did accomplish the unbelievable feat of keeping me from reaching my climax not quite yet.

Chase finally pushed his red-hot poker against my puckered hole, splitting my anal ring and driving himself into me. He did it in perfect syncopation with his thrusting hips, not missing a beat in his execution.

Groaning into the comforter, I shut my eyes and enjoyed the feeling of that giant pole splitting me in half as it slid inside me. His velvety head punched my prostate as he buried to the hilt in me.

McIntyre commanded, "Now, Brand."

That was a good thing, because I was unable to hold back my climax any longer. I felt the hot cum pump from the head of my cock as I rocked back onto Master's big pole. His pubic hairs were tickling my ass cheeks at the very moment that I felt my hole lock down on his cock. His thick legs were holding my legs together, making me even tighter than ever.

"Oh, fuck, Brand," Master groaned. "How in the fuck do you stay so Goddamn tight?"

"I could ask you how you stay so Goddamn hard after coming twice already, Master." I moaned, my voice husky and raw.

"You do it for me, Brand. I don't know what else to say about it."

"You don't need to say anything, Master."

And he didn't. McIntyre put his palms down flat on the small of my back, pressed down, and fed me his giant hose again and again. By the time he was ready to come, he had moved his hands up to my shoulder blades, was leaning over me, and fucking drilling my upturned ass. He came in a huge explosion, filling me with more of his sweet cream and groaning through it.

He hooked his thumb back into my mouth and asked, "Who keeps you filled with spunk?"

"You do, Master. You always do, Master."

"That's right." He lay down on top of me, his hairy chest tickling my back and his big cock throbbing away inside me like his heartbeat.

"Master, do you think you will eventually grow tired of this?"

"Fuck, no! You?"

"Never, Master. Do you think it will always be like this?"

"Yes . . ." His voice sounded sleepy.

"Do you promise, Master?"

"I promise. I'm signing a contract locking me into two years, aren't I?" He twisted to the side so that I could see part of his face. His dark hair was messed up on top, making him look super-hot.

"I hope so, Master."

"Monday morning . . ."

"What? You didn't tell me that, Master."

"Marsh just heard from The Service. They want to send a lawyer to us on Monday morning to take care of it."

"And you're okay with all of this, Master?"

"I'm more than okay with it. It's what I want." He chuckled, surprising himself with his own words.

"It's what I want, too, Master, more than anything else in the world."

CHAPTER NINETEEN

The boys were excited the next day when I told them the news about The Service. I had slept almost until lunch time and had gone straight to the hot tub to soak my sore body. McIntyre had outdone himself last night after our talk, making sure that he scratched that itch in my ass as many times as I could handle it.

"Master had to go meet his agent," Braden informed me.

"I don't know where McIntyre is," I added.

"I think I saw him with his gym bag, leaving a little while ago," Jeremy said, leaning over the bar in the kitchen, watching Alex make chicken salad.

Alex turned towards me and said, "Man, Brand, I don't know how you do it."

"Do what?" I asked innocently.

"Take Chase McIntyre's giant cock every day . . ."

I laughed, saying, "Oh, yeah, that."

"He is so fucking big. I couldn't even take all of him yesterday, and I felt like I had been fucked with a baseball bat this morning."

"And that was just once," I said with a smirk.

"Exactly!" Alex agreed, starting to laugh.

Braden piped up, saying, "McIntyre scares me."

"Really?" I asked.

"He's absolutely drop-dead handsome, but dangerous-looking," Braden said, saying more words in a row than I had ever known him to say. "Like a big black bear."

"Dangerous?" I repeated, floored by that word.

"Scary dangerous . . . intimidating dangerous, not hurtful dangerous," he corrected.

"Fuck, he even scares me, Brand," Jeremy said. I looked at Alex, who just shook his head. "I mean, he's hotter than hell, but he's so intense towards you that it's scary."

"If you think he's intense normally, just wait until he fucks you. That's when he is super laser-focused," Alex said with a weird look on his face.

"What's wrong?" Jeremy asked with a chuckle. "You don't want to give it another try, Alex?"

Alex hadn't been very effusive since I had met him, but he was animated about this subject. "Hell, no. No offense, Brand."

"None taken," I said immediately.

He continued, "I mean, if Master wants me to fuck with McIntyre again, I will. But I'm perfectly content letting Brand have his man."

"And I'm so cool with that . . ."

We laughed and talked as we ate lunch. Master had left a note saying that he wanted to get the four of us on a workout plan and into the gym this afternoon. We were all excited to know more about his charity event tomorrow and hoped that he would open up about it once we got him into the gym.

The workout that afternoon was good, but left me sorer than I had ever been before. All of us came home and soaked in the hot tub, trying to keep the fatigue out of our muscles. McIntyre came in right before dinner, took one look at my workout program on the counter and scoffed.

"Is this what you think you are going to get by with, Brand?" His light-grey eyes bored into my green ones.

"No, sir. It is the plan that Master came up for me." Marshall was on the phone and was paying us no attention.

Chase threw the paper down on the counter and said, "Well, that's not going to happen. I will make corrections to this tomorrow."

Jeremy, Alex, and Braden all looked terrified.

Chase noticed the other Servants for a change and quickly added, "For Brand only, of course."

"Of course," I repeated drolly, while rolling my eyes.

McIntyre stared at me like he could burn a hole in my soul. "One," he said firmly.

A chill ran up my spine and my crotch felt hot as fire at the exact same moment. I lowered my head and tried to catch my breath. Chase McIntyre could absolutely command my body now with one simple word. It was terrifying and electrifying to me all at the same time, just like that chill and fire trick he just made my body do.

"Sorry, sir," I said, finding the courage to look back up at him.

"That's what I thought."

Master put his phone in his pocket and we all sat down at the table to eat. He had promised to tell us about the New York Shadow Ball being held tomorrow over dinner, so we all were anxious to start eating. After Marshall finished his salad, he began to talk.

"The Shadow Ball is for a charity that I care a lot about," he began. "It's held in a big industrial space that they transform into a series of rooms and corridors. It is a two-fold kind of experience for the men who pay a lot to come to the ball. First, they get a chance to fuck with you guys, and I want to thank you in advance for that."

"Our pleasure, Master," I said quickly.

"It will be their pleasure as well, Brand. Secondly, the men will get to meet the famous Masters and spend time with us in a big cocktail party setting."

"Why is it called the Shadow Ball, Master?" Jeremy asked.

"It's dark and seedy," Chase said before shoving some roasted eggplant into his mouth.

Master looked at him and said, "It is supposed to simulate those illegal Service Stations that allow customers to interact with the . . . clients. Don't you guys worry, you will be perfectly safe, and the men will not know who you are or which celebrity you belong to. This will be the first time that Mac and I will be in the lounge."

I hadn't thought that McIntyre would be included in that part, so I quickly looked up at him.

Master spoke for him, "Yes, Brand, I have included you in the program as Chase McIntyre's Servant."

"Awesome, Master, thank you."

"Will we be anonymous because it is so dark, Master?" Alex asked.

"That, and the fact that you will be masked."

"Masked?" I blurted out, causing McIntyre to glare at me and hold two thick fingers up to his chest. My balls responded to his gesture with that familiar twinge of passion igniting in my balls.

"Yes, this year the theme is to wear Mexican wrestling masks. That way the Masters can identify their Servants, but no one else can," Taylor answered me. He jumped up from the table and disappeared down the hallway. Returning with a Fed-ex package, he ripped it open and pulled out four shiny colorful masks. "They glow in the dark."

Jeremy, Alex, Braden, and I each grabbed one, admiring them. They were all green and gold, but with different patterns to them. I tried it on and found it to not be unpleasant. The eye and mouth holes were large, so I didn't get a panicky feeling like I had once at The Service Academy when a latex fetish mask had been strapped onto my head. My mask was mostly green, but had yellow sparkly pieces that formed a bulls-eye on the forehead that radiated over my head and across my face.

"This should be fun," McIntyre commented before stuffing

some grilled salmon into his mouth.

"It should be," Master agreed. "And it will raise a lot of money for the soldiers."

"That makes it all worth it," a normally quiet Braden stated.

McIntyre punished me for my outbursts later that night, informing me that he was going to leave me alone tomorrow, since I would need to be on top of my game for the Shadow Ball. It was not what I wanted, of course, but I saw the sense of it. The fucking that I received after my punishment was one of the greatest exhibitions of ass pounding that I had ever seen or been a part of.

It caused me to ask McIntyre, "Are you afraid someone will fuck better than you tomorrow, Master?"

"What do you think?" he said, smirking harder than ever.

"Not a chance, is what I think."

"You are mine. It doesn't matter what happens tomorrow, you are mine and will always be mine."

"Yes, sir!"

"I will be the one that gives you what you need, no matter what anyone else does. Do you understand?"

"Yes, sir. No one can give me what you do."

"That's right. Now let's get some sleep. You're going to need to get a lot of rest tomorrow before we go."

"Yes, Master." I yawned, falling asleep against his big chest almost immediately.

The next morning, we all slept in and even took a nap in the afternoon, before the charity event. Pasta was on the menu for dinner to give us some extra energy for the night. We spent most of the rest of the afternoon bathing and manscaping so that we represented our Masters well. Taylor told us to wear jockstraps, shorts, and t-shirts, since we would be changing in the car.

I finished preening, dressed, told Jeremy that I was going to wait downstairs, and left our bedroom, closing the door behind me. McIntyre was coming out of his room at the same time, and I was floored to see that he was wearing a tuxedo, looking very stylish and very handsome. His hair was spiked to perfection, and his square jaw was freshly shaven.

"Master," I sighed, my voice all heady with lust.

"Servant," he returned with a smirk.

"You look fantastic, Master."

"Thank you, Brand."

"The things I wouldn't do for you in that tux, Master," I said suggestively, raising an eyebrow.

"It takes a tux to get you to do those things, young one?"

I swallowed hard as he moved his body up against mine, pinning me to the hallway wall. "No, sir. You know I would do anything for you, Master, don't you?"

McIntyre chuckled, turned my body, grabbed my ass, and ushered me down the hallway. "Yes, that I know, Brand." We hit the stairs and he turned back to me and said, "Staying away from you today was a feat . . ."

"For me, too, Master."

"I won't be kept at bay when this event is over. Do you understand?"

I swallowed hard again. "Yes, Master."

"I might just have to fuck you all night long to make up for lost time . . ."

"Will you wear the tux, Master?"

"If you want me to, I will." He laughed at the thought of it. We joined Braden, who was sitting on one of the couches and waiting.

When everyone was ready, Taylor ushered us out of the house, and I was surprised to see a stretch limo idling in front of the house. Master smiled as he held the door open for us and we piled into the back. We had glasses of champagne, toasting our good luck, our famous Masters, and the exciting Shadow Ball.

The limo stopped at the loading dock of a warehouse which was dark and dirty. For the first time it hit me that this wasn't going to be as glamorous as I had envisioned. Master reached into an inside coat pocket and pulled a small envelope out. He poured the contents into his hand. I was far enough away that I could only see the gleam of gold. Opening his fingers wide, his palm held four tiny locks, each one with a golden key inserted in the bottom.

"Put on your masks and strip to your jocks," Master commanded.

Before donning my bulls-eye mask, I watched as Marshall handed one lock and key to my true Master. I pulled down the zipper in the back, noticing for the first time that there was a latch at the bottom.

Marshall fastened the latch on the back of Braden's mask and inserted the lock, pulling the key out and putting it in his pocket.

McIntyre pulled me into the floorboards in front of him. Whispering into my ear through the fabric, he said, "Make me proud tonight, Brand."

"Yes, sir."

He placed the lock on my mask and the key into his jacket pocket.

I removed my shorts carefully in the cramped space, and McIntyre pulled my t-shirt over my head. He reached around me, pinched my nipples, and whispered, "Remember what I said about after this is over . . ."

I felt the blood immediately start to rush to my cock. If McIntyre only knew that I would never be able to forget those words, because they were emblazoned on my memory bank . . .

Instead of admitting that to him, I simply said, "Yes, sir."

CHAPTER TWENTY

W e were a strange-looking group walking up that loading dock—two Masters in tuxedos and four of us Servants, completely naked except for flip flops, jock straps, and Mexican wrestling masks. Our green and gold masks glowed in the dark of the sheltered dock.

Once inside, we were met by some of the charity organizers, who ushered our Masters into one room and the four of us Servants into another one. It was a large room that looked like it might have been a big freezer at one point. The charity organizers had equipped it with lush carpet and big leather sofas. There were around thirty Servants already there, lounging in their glittery masks which were brilliant blues, purples, oranges, reds, yellows, pinks, eerie whites, beautiful golds, and sparkly silvers.

The Servants were very interested in the four of us walking in. Not many Masters were able to afford two Servants, let alone four. They greeted us warmly and had a lot of questions for us. Most of them, of course, had no idea who our Master was until we told them and then explained who he was.

"The NOMARs are going to have a feast tonight!" I exclaimed, looking around at all the different body types and shapes that were around. All of us had good bodies, even though there were multiple types—stocky, skinny, tall, short, muscular, thick and flabby, hairy, smooth, tattooed, as well as every ethnicity that one could want.

"Yeah, they are!" a tall guy in a gold and white mask said to me. His eyes were dark and his skin was tan. "Did your

Master tell you what we would be doing?"

"Fucking," I said plainly. I saw that several more Servants were ushered into the room.

"Yeah, I know that, but the details . . ." He was interrupted by one of the organizers who was calling us to attention.

"Looks like we are about to find out," I said to him over the murmurs from the crowd.

The organizer addressed us, saying, "We're going for a little walk through to show you guys what is offered this year and then we will have a drawing to see who goes where. Follow me." He turned and exited through a curtain.

We scrambled to follow him. There were close to fifty of us now.

"This year we have five rooms for the guests to visit. This first one is called *X Marks the Spot*." He opened a door and we went into a carpeted room full of full-sized X-shaped supports. They had cardboard cutouts of Servants attached to where we would be strapped. Some Servants would be upside down, some right side up, and some on their sides. We looked around and then followed the organizer out.

Not bad, but I'm sure this position would get pretty boring after a while.

"Here in the hallway, between the rooms, we will have bouncers." These turned out to be armchairs for the NOMARs to sit in, and Servants were suspended on bungie cords above them. The idea was that the NOMAR could pull the Servant down into their laps. "And we will also have portable coffee tables." He indicated a padded square on wheels where a cardboard Servant was strapped to each side. It was taller than a coffee table, putting your mouth and your asshole at exactly the right height to be fucked by most men.

I knew right away that I did not want either of those two jobs.

The organizer showed us to the next room, calling it *Slingsational*. It was a room full of slings and swings hung at various heights and positions around the room. The next room was called the *Wheel of Fortune*. It was a giant roulette wheel with Servants strapped into a variety of positions. It would spin after a certain amount of time for variety.

This was definitely a possibility for me, since I enjoyed the chance aspect of it, but I wondered if the spinning would make me sick.

The fifth room was called *The Conveyor Belt*. This one required the NOMARs to get into the action, being suspended above a conveyor belt on a bungied harness. The Servants were strapped to the conveyor belt in various positions and would slowly move from one NOMAR to the next. I liked the idea of this one a lot and decided to pick it, unless the last room was more spectacular.

The last room looked like a giant spider's lair when we went in, and I was a little frightened at first. It was called *Cocoon*. The entire room held mesh net columns that went from floor to ceiling. Servants were strapped inside the mesh nets, suspended from the ceiling by manacles and attached to the floor by them, as well. I could immediately see why a NOMAR would like this room, but for the Servant I bet it would pull on your arms, wrists, and shoulders terribly. I did not want this room.

The organizer showed us the NOMARs locker room next, where they would get showered and dressed afterwards. From the locker room, there was a door that led to the *Celebrity Lounge,* where our Masters would be waiting to meet and greet the guests.

He then led us back to our waiting room, telling us that there would be breaks every so often for short amounts of time. We each put our names on a slip of paper and put it into a jar. We were instructed to use our first name and our Master's last name. I hesitated at first, not knowing whether to use Taylor or McIntyre, but decided on *Brand McIntyre.*

The organizer shook the jar and began to pull names out of it and assign jobs. He did this very quickly, handing out rubber arm bracelets that had the name of the assignment on it as he went along. My name was called early and I picked the Conveyor Belt. Jeremy got the sling room, Alex took the *X Marks the Spot* room , and we all waited for Braden's name to be called. It wasn't until next to last.

I felt badly for him, as he had a choice of being on a portable coffee table or the *Cocoon* room. He picked the rolling table and the other three of us went over to console him.

We were told to lube ourselves, and once we had done so, were immediately taken to our assignments. There were seven of us attached to the conveyor belt. The organizer asked each of us what our specialty was and then strapped us accordingly. Two Servants had their mouths over the target, one Servant their hands, two their asses while they knelt, and me and another guy were strapped down on our backs with our legs pulled back over our chests. At least the belt was padded and the straps were soft. I knew we were going to be here a while. The operator ran the belt, showing us what it would be like. When I got to the end of the belt and flipped over to the bottom, it was a weird experience, but it gave me something different to look at and feel, so I was good with it.

A clock somewhere chimed the hour and the operator yelled, "Show time!" and disappeared behind the machinery.

The door soon opened, and shadowy figures moved up the metal staircase to the platform above us. There was room on the platform for multiple men to stand and watch. The platform was dark, the only lights being on the conveyor belt itself, pointing right at us.

The operator came onto the platform above us, explaining what to do if they wanted to participate. Some of the men laughed out loud when they heard what was going to happen and some seemed to be excited to get started.

"My two boys and I will do it," a voice called out in the darkness.

"I'm in, too!" a deep voice responded.

"I'll give it a shot . . ."

The operator showed them how to strap into the harnesses, and then the machinery whirred to life, lowering the five NOMARs towards us. As they got right above us, I could start to make out details like the five hard cocks that were pointed down at us. I was in position number five, so I would be on top of the conveyor belt for a while.

As the harnessed man descended towards me, he blocked the spotlight from my eyes, which allowed me to see the details of this man. He was tall with a shaved head. He had a dark black beard that started next to his ears and completely covered his jaw. The hair on his face contrasted sharply with the rest of his body, which was smooth and hairless except for his pubic hair and armpit hair. His body was a model of physical perfection. He had a giant thick chest with big pecs. His biceps were gigantic, as well as his thighs. He was so big, that I hoped that the harness would hold him.

I watched, fascinated, as he guided his cock into my upturned hole. His piston was unusually short, but thick. When he entered me, I felt my anal ring stretch wide around that fireplug.

"Hi," he said, awkwardly, once his crotch was resting on my upturned ass.

"Sir," I said matter-of-factly. I could see the Servant to the right of me on the conveyor belt and watched him swallow a big, thick, dark dick into the mouth hole of his wrestling mask.

"I'm . . . not used . . . to being able to see you . . ." He was struggling with his words.

"You can just fuck me, sir." I saw the look on his face turn to embarrassment. I was quick to add, "Before the machine turns the belt."

I saw the realization cross his face and then he said, "Oh, yeah." He started to fuck with all the grace of a power lifter doing a squat press, but he was very enthusiastic about it. Before long, an amber strobe light came on with a machinery sound. The strobe light was on a long pole like you see at construction sites.

Suddenly the conveyor belt jumped to life and started to move me down the line to the next spot. Muscle-guys' cock popped out of my tight hole, and I enjoyed seeing the shocked look on his face as I rolled away from him.

The next guy that I rolled under I saw was Indian as the belt stopped in the perfect position. He was probably in his late thirties, also with a black beard and a thick chest. Unlike the first guy, this one had a totally furry chest, belly, arms, and legs. His dark eyes reflected the light as he guided his big cock to my puckered hole.

Something about him struck me as military. I wasn't sure if it was his square jaw or his military high-and-tight haircut. He was also pretty methodical in his fucking, not wasting any time or energy. He had braced his feet on the belt and was fucking that big lap-hog into me at a good pace.

I was almost sorry to see the strobe light come on when it did. As I moved away from the current guy, I noticed that the number of men on the platform above us had increased, and they were shouting their approval. They went especially wild when the Indian guy's dick pulled out of my ass with a giant popping sound.

The next guy I rolled under was the dad here with his two sons. I couldn't see the details of the sons, but their dad was overweight with a big, fat, hairy belly and a dark shadow of a beard on his face. He was not attractive, but not ugly either. He had an average-sized wand that was thick and crowned with a big mushroom cap of a head.

He slid himself into me and buried in all the way, before leaning over me and yelling at his kids. "Hey boys, wait to you feel this one! He's tight as a virgin!"

"Loosen him up for us then, Pop!" came the reply out of the darkness.

Pop got to work, putting on a fucking show for his boys. I got the impression from the moans and grunts to my right that neither of the boys was watching or paying attention to anything other than their dicks getting serviced.

His big cockhead cleaned out my pipes and prodded my prostate, which felt good. I closed my eyes and laid my head back on the padded belt and tried to wait for the strobe light to activate. My mind wandered to how my friends were faring in their various jobs. Flashing lights alerted me to the fact that we were about to change.

I moved down to the dad's youngest son. He must have been a teenager, from the looks of him. I only knew that he was the youngest son because I got a glimpse of my next guy, and he was at least twenty years old. Both sons looked like their father, but younger and in better shape. Both of them had inherited the same big cockhead from their father. This youngest son fumbled with his cock, which was very skinny and missed my hole several times before sinking into me.

He was nervous and sweating profusely.

I whispered, "Take it easy. Take your time. It's going to be all right."

He smiled down at me and said, "It's the first time I've ever fucked while someone was watching. I've only been to Service Stations before."

"You're doing fine," I said, lying back and squeezing his cock with my ass muscles to give him some encouragement.

He took a deep breath and got busy fucking. He didn't last long, blowing his load into me within a minute. He got congratulatory shout-outs from his Pop and his older brother. He collapsed on top of me, barely held above me by his harness and quietly said, "Thanks."

"No problem."

"Now what do I do, Dad?" he asked.

"Let this next guy clean you up," his father told him.

The strobe light signaled the next move, and I slid under the older brother, who inserted his long, big-headed cock right into my tight hole.

"Jesus, he's tight," he told his relatives.

"Jesus, you're long," I parlayed back.

He looked down at me as he started to hip-thrust his trouser trout into me. "I'm not used to my holes talking back."

"I'm not used to being referred to as a hole," I shot back.

"It's a pretty fantastic hole," he said, backing off from his sharp tone.

"Thanks."

"You gonna tell me who you belong to?" He seemed a little insistent, almost pushy, to the point it raised alarm bells.

"Nope."

"C'mon. I bet you wish I was your Master and that you got this long cock on a daily basis."

"Oh, buddy. I'm so sorry. I'm getting your cock right now, but all I can think about is being with my Master tonight." Fortunately for me, the strobe light turned on and I rotated over the edge of the belt and hung upside down, enjoying the feeling of being by myself for a change.

CHAPTER TWENTY-ONE

When I was hanging under the conveyor belt, I heard the NOMARs being hauled back up to the platform. I'm sure that there were five more guys waiting to take their place. It sounded like the platform was full of shouting guys. A group of three guys began to unstrap us from the belt, giving us the first break. I didn't need to use the bathroom like some of the guys, but I did need to stand and stretch my legs.

The time went by pretty quickly, even though it was a lot longer than the three minutes that they had told us about. Some of the Servants switched positions, but I wanted to stay the course. Soon we were all strapped in again and I rotated up onto the top of the belt.

The NOMARs were lowered towards us. I saw a strange red glow at the top of the one above me and a huge, white cock at the other end, causing me to swallow a little before he landed on top of me. Now that he was closer, I could see that he was in his fifties, had hair in a ring around his head, a salt-n-pepper goatee and mustache and a thick body. His skin was so white that I thought it probably had never seen the light of day. The red glow I had seen was the lit end of a big cigar that he had clamped between his teeth.

He wasted no time in hunching over me and blasting my anal ring apart with his huge white bratwurst. He kept pushing into me until he was buried to the nuts inside me.

"Fuck me!" He groaned.

I shifted my ass in the harness, trying to get some relief from the pressure he was exerting on me.

He looked in my eyes and said, "You just come on duty, bud?"

"No, sir."

"You're a Servant?"

"Yes, sir."

"Your Master fucks you every day?" He pulled all of the way out of me and then slammed back in.

I bit my lip, bracing myself against his thrust. "Yes, sir." I thought it was none of his business, but since he didn't know who I was, I thought it was safe to answer.

"Then how are you so fucking tight?" He pulled all the way out of me again before slamming back into me.

"I seem to be able to take your fat baby-maker without a problem!" I snorted.

"And a mouth on you, as well." He pulled back out and then exploded back into me again. He raised his voice and turned his head to the side saying, "Sam, Dave, this one's the one we want!"

What the fuck is he talking about?

"How do you know, Bill?"

"Just you wait and you'll know! His mask is green with a yellow bulls-eye!"

I was left to wonder what he was talking about and why he was describing my mask while he started to fuck in earnest. He was huge, stretching my ass around his thick cock and setting my ass on fire as it slid up and down his shaft. He was no Chase McIntyre, but he certainly knew how to fuck.

The strobe light suddenly lit up the dark room, and the conveyor belt moved me down to Bill's friend, who also was smoking a big stogie. When I stopped under him, I realized that he must have been Bill's brother, because they looked so much alike.

"Bill's brother?" I asked. He was completely bald with no facial hair and probably in his forties. He was thick and muscled, with the same pale skin as his brother Bill.

"Yeah, Sam," he said, feeding his cock into my ass with one hand and holding his cigar with the other one. It was not as thick or as long as his brother's, but it was nice. "That's our other brother over there," he indicated with a jerk of his head.

"Cool," I said, not knowing what else to say.

"Bill, you're right! His ass is so fucking fantastic!" he yelled to his brother.

"Why don't you get to fucking it then?" I asked, figuring that if they liked my smart mouth, I would give it to them.

Sam bore down on me, giving me a great ride before the strobe light interrupted him. "God Dammit!" he yelled as I rolled out from under him.

"Sorry, Sam," I teased him as I stopped under his brother.

Dave was a slightly smaller version of Sam, bald and thick with a full blond beard that framed his face beautifully. He looked like he was in his late thirties and had inherited all of the family's good looks. His skin was less white and his muscles were better defined.

"Hi Dave," I said, flirting with him a little bit.

"What's up?" he asked around his cigar, dropping some ash on my stomach as he dipped his head to watch his cock furrow into my sore hole. Dave's cock was very skinny and average in length, but I was enjoying him in a whole host of other ways.

"Oh, fuck," he groaned as my still-tight hole wrapped itself around his hot cock.

In the darkness, I heard Bill yell out, "Is he still so God damn tight, Dave?"

"Yeah, he's squeezing the shit out of my Johnson!" Dave yelled back. "He's the one, all right!" he said more to himself, than to me. Dave fucked with force, causing me to have to hold onto his big biceps hanging below the harness as he rocked me.

The strobe light came on much too fast, and I was whisked

away to an elderly black daddy who had a cock like a snake, long and thin. I used my time fantasizing about what my Master might do to me tonight and whether he would approve of Dave joining us.

The belt moved me down to a nerdy little guy who looked like an accountant. He had an enormous cock and didn't say a word the whole time he fucked me with it. He was out of practice, but settled in quickly to a good pace. I shook my head as he punched my prostate over and over and reminded myself that I couldn't judge a book by its cover.

When the amber light lit up the dark room, I was happy to roll underneath the conveyor belt and get a break. It had been a really long night already and I had one more round to go on the conveyor belt. My legs were so stiff when the handlers released me that I spent the first half minute stretching them out. Once I felt like I could move safely again, I quickly went to the restroom.

The hallway was dark as death when I stepped into it. I could hear the noises of sex happening all around me, but could see nothing. The restroom was right beside the Conveyor Belt room, so I turned and felt for it. Almost simultaneously, my left hand grasped the door latch and my right hand landed on a sturdy chest.

Jerking back quickly, I opened the door, letting light spill out into the dark. The chest belonged to Bill, the older brother from my recent turn on the conveyor belt. He had his arms crossed and had a really mean look on his face.

"Hey there, boy," he leered.

I tried to remove my hand, but he grabbed my wrist and held it hard. My first reaction was to scream, but I stopped myself.

"Where you going in such a hurry?" His tone was unremarkable, but I could sense the threat in his words.

"I only have one minute before I have to go back," I

mumbled. I knew I was supposed to use the title of sir when addressing a NOMAR for this event, but he was hurting my wrist, so therefore, in my mind, he didn't deserve the use of the title.

His mean look turned into a really creepy smile as he said, "I just wanted to tell you how much I enjoyed you tonight, boy. That's all." He let go of my wrist and melted back into the shadows.

I was completely shaken up when I approached the toilet stall. Wiping some of the lube and cum off of my ass with toilet paper, I pulled my jock to the side and began to relieve myself. I was so on edge that when the door opened and a body approached me from behind, I almost jumped out of my skin. Realizing that whoever it was had not gone into a stall and was probably standing right behind me, I balled my fist up, quickly spun around and awkwardly swung in the small space.

A big hand engulfed my fist and stopped it in midair without hurting me. I jerked my head up and looked into my Master's light-grey eyes. With a heavy sigh, I lunged forward and collapsed into his tuxedoed chest. His big arms wrapped around me.

"Brand, what's wrong?" McIntyre's deep voice rumbled through his chest, giving me instant comfort.

I wrapped my arms around him and held him tight, saying, "Nothing really. Some jerk was creeping on me, Master."

He pulled me back away from him so he could look at me. His face held a look of disbelief. "And you were frightened?" His eyes held mine in his laser-like gaze, daring me to not be honest with him.

The last thing in the world I wanted to do was to disappoint him. "Yes, sir. Only after he grabbed me, Master."

His face clouded with anger immediately and he set his lips in a determined position. "Did he hurt you?"

"No, Master."

"Who is he? I will take care of that asshole."

I didn't want McIntyre to get into trouble, and I was feeling better, so I blew it off saying, "I don't know . . . some asshole. Wait a minute, what are you doing back here, Master?"

"Checking up on you, of course." He smirked.

"Good thing . . ."

"Good thing," he repeated, starting to laugh.

"I have to go, Master. I'm out of time."

"I'm not used to you telling me what you are going to do," he smirked. "I'll walk you back."

I felt completely safe with this man, like I had a personal superhero on my side.

"I kinda like bossing you around . . ." I held my breath waiting for his response.

It was so dark that I couldn't see his face, but his deep voice rang out. "I will punish you right here in front of everyone."

"I would like that, Master . . . but I have a job to do for charity, so you will just have to schedule an appointment for that later. I will have my people call your people."

He actually snorted as we were heading back to the conveyor belt. "My staff is going to come into contact with you, that is for sure."

That made me laugh.

Master asked, "Are you performing at your best?"

"Yes, Master."

He knew immediately that I was lying. "Really, Brand?"

Sighing deeply, I amended my answer. "Mostly, Master. It is hard not to daydream of what you have planned for us later."

He cracked a huge grin that reflected the dim light of the dark room. "I have distracted you from this task with my future plans. I will rectify that for the next time."

"Yes, sir."

"You have one more run of the belt, and then you will come to me in the lounge."

"Yes, sir."

"And then we will leave and you will see what happens to you when I am unable to have my way with you for a whole day."

His words did nothing but figuratively set me on fire, causing my dick to start to poke its head out of the fabric of my jock strap.

"Make me proud, Brand."

"Always, Master."

"Don't just try, do it!"

I watched as he disappeared into the gloomy darkness.

The belt operator was a little pissed that I had been gone for so long, telling me about it as he strapped me into place in the seventh spot this time. Five of my other fellow Servants were already on the belt, performing. I would have to wait upside down until two of them had rotated down to the underside.

And that was okay with me, because I was going to need some time to get my head back on straight. After that interaction with my Master, I couldn't get the image of my new Master out of my head or the smell of him out of my nose. Everything about him screamed *man* and I was all about it. He was my superhero, my Master, and my world. He was everything I had dreamed a Master would be and so much more. I knew at that point, hanging upside down on a conveyor belt, that I needed Chase McIntyre just as much as I needed to breathe.

CHAPTER TWENTY-TWO

The last trip down the conveyor belt seemed to take an eternity. One of the NOMARs was a talker who wanted to ask me a million questions, which was really annoying, considering that I only wanted to fantasize about what McIntyre would be doing to me when this was over. The other guys were cool, but couldn't hold my interest. I had to admit that each time I moved a spot down the belt, I got more and more excited.

The man in the last harness got the best of me, because I was so excited that I couldn't lie still. I rocked myself back and forth to match his thrusts, causing him to explode with his climax long before the amber strobe light signaled my departure over the edge.

The first five Servants had all been released by the time I flipped upside down and the operator was working on releasing the guy beside me. He got down with a heavy sigh, bending at the waist to stretch his back. The operator was busy fiddling with the straps and watching the Servant stretch.

"Hey, buddy. How about getting me down from here? I got places to go!" I regretted saying it as soon as it was out of my mouth. I saw the look on his face and knew he wasn't going to hurry.

He unstrapped my legs and then said, "I'll be right back." He disappeared into the darkness.

"Fuck me," I said to myself, hanging my head.

"That's exactly what we had in mind."

The voice came out of the darkness and caused the hairs on

my arms to stand on end. I knew it was Bill and his brothers before they even moved into the circle of light where I could see them. They looked formidable.

"The guy from the charity will be right back," I said as confidently as my voice allowed.

"Yeah, but no," Sam said. "We offered a few bills, and he is taking a smoke break."

"Get him down from up there," Bill told his two younger brothers. "But make sure you hold him tight. I have a feeling he is a fighter."

Sam and Dave started to unfasten the straps that held me in place and then lowered me to the ground. I tried to jerk away from their big hands on my arms, but was unable to break their grip on me.

I turned my attention to Bill and said, "My Master will be here in a couple of seconds, and he will fucking kill you if you lay a hand on me." My voice dripped with venom.

All three of them chuckled and Dave asked, "Who is your Master?"

"None of your fucking business!" I spit at him.

"Fiery," Sam commented.

"Let's go before someone comes," Bill said. "Ricky, get out here."

Now, I was really confused. Who the fuck was Ricky? I saw a form step forward from the murk and saw that it was a Servant in a jock with a brilliant red wrestling mask with blue wings on it.

"See here, this is our Servant, Ricky. He's going to fill in for you to keep your Master at bay so that my brothers and I can scooch you off with us."

Oh, fuck! It was worse than I thought. They weren't just going to fuck me, they were going to take me away. My heart started pounding and it felt like I couldn't catch my breath.

"Get his mask off, Dave."

I watched as Bill took a golden key out of his pocket and took Ricky's mask off. Dave wrenched the lock on the back of my mask while I tried to fight him. Sam held my masked head between his hands and squeezed.

I heard a hard popping sound and then my mask was off. I felt even more exposed than I ever had.

"He's not bad looking," Dave said in surprise.

"Much better than that cum pig, Ricky," Sam chimed in.

"Get them switched," Bill said sternly.

I had a fleeting note of sympathy for Ricky, that they were treating him this way. But at the same time, I was too busy feeling sorry for myself to worry about anyone else. I watched in disgust as the boys took a roll of packing tape and taped my mouth closed.

Much to my surprise, they also taped Ricky's mouth. I was left wondering until they switched our masks and locked mine back on. They had cut through my lock, so they were unable to lock Ricky's mask, but put some tape on it to hold it in place.

While they worked on Ricky's new mask, I had the chance to notice that Ricky was tall like me and had a similar build. He would probably have a good chance to pass as me, but what these people didn't realize was that Chase would know immediately. I was confident in that.

While they were focused on Ricky, I tried one last trick and broke free from Dave. I tried to run, but didn't get very far before I was knocked down by one of them. Bill pulled me to my feet and slapped me across the mask.

"Try that again and we'll fucking hurt you." What frightened me the most in that statement was how calmly he said it. It was so scary that I immediately told myself to be more careful from now on.

The three brothers tied my hands behind my back, making sure that they were securely held in place.

"Go now and let him see your mask in the lounge," Bill told Ricky. Then he turned to me, grabbed my bicep, and ushered me out into the now-dimly lit hallway. Instead of going to the lounge with everyone else, we headed for the loading dock door that I had entered through so many hours ago.

We were immediately stopped at the door by security. Bill showed his ID and then the guards looked at an *iPad*. It occurred to me as both guards looked at the screen and then at me that they were looking at my mask to make sure that Bill had the right Servant.

I tried to get their attention through the tape over my mouth, but Bill just talked loudly, making smart-ass comments to the guards about what a poor job I had done and that I was going to need to be punished when they got me home. The guards, being horned-up NOMARs themselves, laughed and let them through the security checkpoint.

Feeling like this was my last chance, I decided to try to make a break for it again. After watching a million *Criminal Minds* episodes on TV, I was fully aware that if they left the premises with me, it would be much harder to find us. I took a deep breath and abruptly barreled backwards out of Bill's grasp. Knocking down Sam behind me was sheer luck, but it cleared the path back up the stairs and into the building.

Unfortunately for me, I was stopped short by a hand pulling on my bound wrists. It wrenched my shoulders and made me collapse onto my knees. I heard Dave call to the guards, "It's okay. He is just dreading what we have in store for him tonight!"

"I don't blame him!" one of the guards called back.

Dave spoke in my ear, managing to growl, "Nice try! I will break your fucking neck if you try that again and still fuck your tight hole afterwards. Do you understand me?"

Dave lifted me to my feet, causing pain to explode through

my arms and shoulders. He headed me back to the parking lot, and a grey work van drove up to the curb. On the side of the van was the name, *Fizzolli Brothers. Plumbers who always have the right section of pipe.*

Subtle. So these three psychos were plumbers who obviously did well enough to have a Servant of their own. I felt terrible for Ricky and wondered if he had met my Master yet.

The place was crowded, now that the Servants were finished with their parts of the charity event. Most of the celebrities were surrounded by NOMARs fresh out of the showers who were clamoring to meet and talk with them.

McIntyre had been constantly scanning the room since the arrival of the first of the Servants in their brightly colored wrestling masks. He had a terribly uncomfortable feeling until he saw Brand come in through the far doorway. McIntyre could only see his head with the bulls-eye design on the mask as he made his way through the crowd. McIntyre followed the line of his path and smiled when he saw the bar at the end of it.

This was a different experience for Chase McIntyre. He was usually one of the NOMARs who contributed to the charity and then fucked his way through every room until he got to the lounge. He had satisfied himself only three times tonight, so that he could check on Brand the other times. He didn't regret it, finding it odd himself. He never would have imagined that one Servant could have captivated his attention like Brand had.

McIntyre let out a deep breath and for the first time, relaxed as he shook hands and talked idly with the NOMARs who so wanted his attention. He kept constantly checking on Brand's progress, who didn't stray too far from the bar. McIntyre smirked. He thought to himself that if Brand was drunk when this event was over, he was absolutely going to get punished in a major way.

The crowd started to thin, faster than McIntyre imagined it would. But then again, now that he thought about it, rich guys didn't seem to be impressed by celebrity as much as working class dudes. The rich ones were still enamored with the professional athletes though, causing Taylor and his lines to be longer than any of the actors or politicians that were present.

McIntyre wondered why Brand was still at the bar in the back of the room. He was used to Brand being drawn to him like a moth to a flame. A momentary twinge of jealousy ran through him as he considered that maybe Brand was drawn to someone else. Looking over the heads of the crowd, he tried to see if Brand was talking to anyone, but he was too far away. He dismissed this thought immediately, having confidence in what he had with Brand.

Finally the last of his admirers had left, and he watched as the four original Servants of Marshall Taylor headed to the car. McIntyre stepped forward to join them when something unexpected happened to him. Suddenly, right in front of him was a crowd of glittery-masked Servants, anxious to meet him, talk to him, and tell him that they had enjoyed being fucked by him.

He found it flattering, but noticed that for the first time, he wasn't into it. In years past if this would have happened he would have stayed another hour or so, flirting and arranging favors from these Servants' Masters so that he had a constant hole to fuck for the next month. This time, he couldn't wait to avoid them and check on Brand. He greeted them all with a smile while constantly making his way to the exit. He picked up Taylor in the middle of the room and was able to leave most of his fawning admirers behind him.

The limo they had used was one of the last ones left at the curb when the two best friends emerged. The driver held the door open for them and they scrambled in.

McIntyre's gaze immediately went to the Servants, searching for Brand's eyes. Brand was sitting at the far end of the limo with his head facing towards the front.

Why wasn't he looking at me?

And then an internal alarm went off in McIntyre's head. The neck was thick enough, the shoulders were broad enough, but the skin wasn't tan enough.

"Where's Brand?" he shouted at the figure wearing Brand's mask.

Everyone in the limo, who had been talking excitedly, suddenly stopped and stared. The stranger in Brand's mask turned to see what the commotion was, making sure not to make eye contact with anyone.

"He's right there, Mac!" Marshall said, pointing at the fake Brand.

McIntyre leapt forward, scaring everyone. He grabbed the fake Brand by the neck and turned his face to his own. "Who the hell are you and where is Brand?"

When he didn't answer, McIntyre shook him violently. Braden noticed something and put his finger into Ricky's mouth hole. He turned to the rest of the car and said, "His mouth is taped shut."

McIntyre let go of the impostor and dug in his coat pocket for the key. He turned the kid's head, saw the broken lock, and tore through the tape with a single pull. Jerking the mask off, everyone stared at the stranger's face. McIntyre tore the tape off his mouth in one quick movement.

"Who the hell are you?" he growled.

The kid had instinctively raised his hand to his mouth. He looked frightened.

"Well?" Marshall demanded.

"My name is Ricky. Some guy grabbed me and made me trade masks with another marked guy."

"Then why the hell did you pretend to be him? When he

let you go, why didn't you tell someone?" McIntyre was incensed.

"He said he would hurt that kid and my Master if I tried to tell anyone." Ricky's made-up story sounded convincing to most.

"You are in on this!" McIntyre growled. "Where is he?"

"Mac, you don't know that! His mouth was taped . . ."

"He avoided me the whole time we were in the lounge and then he avoided me when we got in the limo. He's in on it. You actively were trying to mislead me!" McIntyre was boiling over with rage.

He lunged at Ricky again as everyone yelled, grabbing him by the throat with one hand and by the ball sack with the other. "I will fucking throttle you, but not until I've ripped your balls and your cock off, so that you can feel it first." He kept his voice calm and monotone, making it even more frightening for Ricky. "Now, you start talking, or I'll start pulling."

Ricky's eyes were quickly going from side to side, looking for help, but there was none. He burst into tears and said with a strained voice, "Okay, okay."

McIntyre loosened his grip on Ricky's neck, but not on his balls.

"My Master commanded me to do it. I didn't want to, but I had no choice. They are far scarier than you are."

Marshall picked his cell phone out of his pocket and said, "I'm calling the police and The Service."

CHAPTER TWENTY-THREE

Lying in the back of the van with my hands tied behind my back and tape on my mouth, I was feeling pretty sorry for myself. The three brothers in the seats at the front of the van, however, were feeling pretty proud of themselves. They were pretty sure that they were going to get away with kidnapping me, but they did not know who they were dealing with.

I could just imagine how furious Chase was going to be when he realized what had happened. He and I had spent so much time together recently that I could picture his reaction and know that I was probably pretty accurate. I knew in my heart that he would never rest until he had me back, and that knowledge gave me hope in this scary situation.

The brother drove for quite a while before pulling off of the highway and into a quiet area which I discovered later was residential. They drug me out of the van and into a house that looked like any other one in the suburbs surrounding New York City. I tried to find something that I could use to identify the house, but there wasn't anything except a house number, which was pretty worthless without the name of the street.

As soon as Bill unlocked the door, I was pushed inside. Dave immediately pulled my jock strap down to my ankles, the tape from my mouth, and the binding from my wrists.

"You will never wear clothes in this house," Sam told me.

I glared at him, and Bill slapped me across the face, hard enough to knock me down. "You will always answer us with *Yes, sir* or *No, sir*."

Grabbing my face, I looked up at him and said, "Yes, sir."

I would be damned if I was going to show them how much I was hurt or how scared I was of them.

"Good," Sam said, pulling me up to my feet. "I'll show you to your room."

"Yes, sir."

I could already see that there was something strange about this house. There was a metal bar that ran the length of the room on the ceiling. As I followed Sam down the hall, the bar continued into each room.

"Bathroom, my room, Dave's room, Bill's room, your room," he pointed out each one. My room was tiny with a King-sized bed taking up most of the space. There was no dresser, no nightstand, no lamp, no artwork on the walls. It was clear that there was only one thing happening in this room, and my heart went out to Ricky once again, wherever he was.

"Yes, sir."

In the corner of the room hung a long flexible cord that was suspended from the rails on the ceiling. I followed the cord down, and on the dusty floor was a collar with a padlock. Sam walked over to it, picked it up, showed it to me, and said, "You might as well get used to wearing it now."

He walked over to me and strapped it onto my neck. Once it was in place, he secured the padlock. "This will allow you access to all the rooms of the house, but will keep you from leaving." Bill and Sam had joined us in the small bedroom.

"Go shower, get cleaned up, and then report to my room," Bill said.

I felt suddenly very nauseous. "Yes, sir." At least in the shower I would be alone for a few minutes and might be able to think of a way out of this mess.

"Everything you need is in there. Get to it!" Sam commanded.

"Yes, sir." I reached up, held the cord above me, and

moved it along the path into the bathroom. There were no doors on any of the rooms, so the shower curtain felt like the most private thing ever. The water wasn't even warm when I stepped into the shower, but I wanted that divider between me and these bad men.

I took my time, scrubbing the night off of me and cleaning myself out with the shower wand. I didn't know how long I could stall, but I definitely was going to push the limits of their patience. I couldn't think of any way that I could escape this nightmare, nor did I see any phones in the house that I possibly could use to call for help.

I was pulled out of my thoughts, literally, when someone jerked on the cord attached to my collar. Turning the water off, I stepped out, used a damp towel to dry myself off, and headed out into the hall. Bill's room was at the end of the hallway, so I walked quietly down towards it.

He was waiting for me when I entered the room. Bill pushed me down onto his bed and growled, "Don't make me wait like that again."

"Yes, sir," I answered, looking around the room and spotting a laptop sitting askew on his dresser. There was a single small lamp on the nightstand that broadcast a little circle of light, but not much.

Bill started to undress. "I'm going to love having you on my cock."

"You might as well enjoy it while you have it. It won't be long before my Master finds me and you three are dead or in jail," I said matter-of-factly.

"I seriously doubt that. You are going to so love getting fucked by me and my brothers that when we decide to let you go, you will not inform on us."

That plan was so far from happening that I burst out laughing before I could stop myself, saying, "Yeah, right!"

Bill immediately back-handed me, breaking my nose.

"You've obviously never been fucked the way you are supposed to be by real men, so you'll see . . ." I could tell from his tone and his facial expression that he believed this to be true. Therefore, there was no sense in arguing with him about it. "Come over here and suck on this." He lifted his big fat cock so that it lay across his fist.

I slid off of the bed and onto my knees in front of him. I had already considered fighting him and refusing to do anything for him, but I got the vibe from Bill and his brothers that they would not hesitate to hurt me, disfigure me, or even kill me if I caused them any trouble. The best plan of action that I could see was to keep them busy, so that it kept them in one place and McIntyre would have an easier time finding me.

As soon as I lifted his bloated cock and sucked it into my hot mouth, he sighed as said, "Atta' boy. Make daddy proud." He reached over to the top of the dresser and grabbed a cigar. He clamped it between his teeth and lit the end.

I could taste the blood from my nose in my mouth.

He was already pretty hard, so I didn't have to do much to excite him. He reached in a drawer and pulled a bottle of lube out and threw it onto the bed. Pulling his big white lap-hog out of my mouth, he slapped me across the face with it several times before climbing onto the bed.

Propping himself up on the headboard, he held his cock up and said, "Come ride Daddy's dick."

"I'll ride your dick, but you will never be my Daddy," I said flatly, climbing onto the bed, straddling his body and sitting on his big white belly.

"You want lube or not?" he threatened.

"Lube please," I grumbled.

Bill slapped me, hard. "Yes, sir."

I glared at him with my most hateful look. "Yes, sir."

He squirted lube on his hand and jacked his cock. I waited patiently for him to lube me, but he skipped it and shoved his white sausage right into me.

It was really hard for me not to close my eyes and imagine that this was my Master underneath me. I longed for McIntyre's big cock inside me, his hairy chest under me, his muscled arms around me, and his handsome face smirking at me. I knew that this whole ordeal would be harder if I let myself fall into that trap, so I kept my eyes open and tried to stay alert.

"Fucking hell! You are so fucking tight."

"Yes, sir."

Bill was starting to breathe heavily and sweat profusely. I put my palms flat down on the top of his chest. His face was starting to turn bright pink under the strain of this fuck, maybe because I wasn't helping at all.

"I could have you ride my fucking pole all night long, you feel so good!" he said, wheezing as he said the words.

"Yes, sir." Suddenly, I thought of something I could do. Slowly, I moved my hands closer together on his clammy chest. His face was getting redder and redder the more he hammered my ass. Soon I had my hands on his breastbone and then, just as he groaned deeply and busted his nut into my ass, I moved my hands to his thick neck and pressed my weight down.

Bill made a choking noise, his eyes widened, and then closed. I felt his body relax while I was on top of him — his chest sagged, his cock shrank and popped out of my ass and his arms fell to his sides. I put my ear to his chest above his heart and heard nothing.

Quickly clamoring off the bed, I kept my eyes on Bill's face.

That was a lot easier and quicker than I thought it would be.

I felt like I had done something terrible, which I had, and for a few seconds I was horrified at myself.

"Snap out of it, Brand." Suddenly, I was channeling Chase McIntyre. He would want me to concentrate on how to get out of this place now that I had an opening. Scrambling over to the laptop, I opened it and saw that it was password protected. I quickly tried all of the brothers' names, first and last and then the full name of their company.

No luck. I sat for a second trying to think of what else it could be when I heard movement in the hallway. Frantically, I shut the laptop and threw the sheet over Bill's apparently lifeless body.

Sam appeared in the doorway, looked at his brother in the bed and said, "He fall asleep on you?"

"After he fucking drilled me," I said with a chuckle. It sounded faked and forced to me, but Sam seemed to buy it.

"Why don't you come to my room then?" he asked.

"Do you want me to shower first and clean up, sir?"

"No, it's okay. Follow me." He turned on his heel and headed for his room.

I sprang into action, the cord holding my collar scraping the rail on the ceiling as I followed him. I gathered the extra cord and looped it around Sam's neck. He immediately grabbed for it and I held it tight with all of my strength. He floundered like a fish out of water, thrashing his legs and kicking the hallway walls.

I didn't know if Dave was asleep or not, but after this skirmish, he would surely be at his brother's side any second. Finally, Sam stopped moving. I was afraid to let him go, but eventually took the pressure off of his neck and he slumped to the floor. Dave never came.

Kicking Sam with my foot to see if he was really out, I decided he should probably be in his bed also, to fool Dave when he woke up. I struggled lifting his big weight, but eventually was able to get him into the bed and covered with a sheet.

Two down and one to go. I tried to sneak across the hall and into Dave's room, but the old floorboards made very loud noises as I went. Dave's room was completely dark and I was almost to his bed when I realized that he wasn't in it.

Where is he? If he's in this house somewhere, wouldn't he have come running to Sam's defense when he was making such a ruckus?

I crept back out into the hallway to make my way to the den or the kitchen when I heard the lock being turned on the front door right in front of me.

Dave walked in with a six pack of beer in one hand and a freshly lit cigarette in his mouth. He took one look at me, saw my guilty face, and said, "What the fuck are you doing?"

CHAPTER TWENTY-FOUR

We had ourselves an old-fashioned standoff — Dave at the door, his keys still hanging from the lock, and me naked in the hall, brain paralyzed.

Dave was the brother that I most needed to sneak up on. He was the youngest and, judging from his muscles, the strongest. But it was too late for that. He was alerted that something was wrong, and I had been caught completely by surprise. My fast thinking in the other two situations had completely left me.

Dave lowered the six-pack of beer, never taking his focus off of me, and rose back up with just one bottle. He smashed it against the door jam and held the broken edge towards me. He advanced, slowly, and I retreated quickly. Dave took one more step towards me and stopped. Then, his body did a really strange thing. His eyes flew open and his body started to jerk.

What the fuck?

I wondered if he was having a seizure. I watched in amazement as he collapsed onto the ratty rug and shook. That's when I saw the silver wires behind him. I followed the wires from his back, out the front door, and into the taser gun of a policeman.

"Thank God!" I said aloud, right before my legs gave out and I sank to the floor.

The cop and his partner stepped into the house. One of them checked on Dave and the other one addressed me, "Are you Brand?"

"Yes, sir." My voice was just as shaky as I felt.

"Where are the other two?" he whispered.

"I think I killed them."

"Where?"

"One is in the bedroom to the left and one in the bedroom at the end of the hall."

"Go outside," he whispered. He didn't realize that the collar around my neck kept me from doing just that, but I did move to the door, where I could keep an eye on the semi-conscious Dave. The officers went down the hallway like silent black shadows. I used my foot to press down on Dave's neck to make sure he didn't move.

I was so nervous that I almost peed myself while I waited. The officers came back down the hallway, clearly more relaxed than before. I could hear more police cars and ambulances arriving, and then I heard a footstep at the door behind me. I whirled around, still on edge, and there he was.

His light gray eyes found mine instantly, even in the dark living room.

"Master!" I croaked. I ran towards him, forgetting about the cord and collar. I was jerked back immediately, hurting my throat and landing on an unconscious Dave.

McIntyre covered the gap between us in one long stride, checking the collar for the release. "I will kill these fuckers."

"I've got bolt cutters in the patrol car. I'll go get them," one of the officers said, taking off. He was back in a flash, cutting through the lock on the back of my collar, freeing me.

"Take him outside and let the paramedics check him out," the other officer told Master. "We've got it from here."

McIntyre pulled me to my feet and I wrapped my arms around his broad chest and held him tightly to me. I breathed in deeply of his smell, enjoying the feeling of being wrapped in his muscular arms again. He ushered me out of the door and down the steps. The paramedics rushed up to me and

Master shrugged them off.

"We have the team doctor here to check on him," McIntyre said as Marshall and a man that I assumed was the doctor came rushing towards us.

"Let us use that stretcher, will you?" the Doctor called out. Soon, he was prying me out of my Master's arms and forcing me down onto the stretcher. My eyes never left McIntyre's face while the doctor poked and prodded me.

"How is he?" McIntyre asked the doctor, the concern for me in his voice warming my naked skin like nothing else could.

"His heart is racing. His blood pressure is way up."

"It's no wonder, he's just been through quite an ordeal," Marshall said.

"I'll give him something to calm his nerves. It will put him out for a little while," the doctor said definitively.

"No. I don't want to be out, Master!" I pleaded with my eyes, as well as my words.

"Brand, it's what is best," he told me in no uncertain terms.

"Master . . ."

"Brand, do as I command you. Let him give you the shot."

"Yes, sir."

The doctor stabbed my arm with the syringe and I quickly fell into a deep sleep.

I was first aware of voices. I couldn't make out what they were saying or who they belonged to, but I definitely could hear voices. Next, I became aware of lying in a very soft bed. I knew I wanted to open my eyes, but I just couldn't bring myself to do it yet.

The fogginess in my head started to clear, and then I was able to identify each voice. The one who spoke now made me hold my breath and started that familiar burning sensation in my balls. It was my Master.

"When I got there he had already subdued two of those assholes and had his foot on the third one's neck. Total badass!"

My eyes flew open and I moaned as I grabbed my head. Whatever that doctor had given me had done a number on my head.

"Brand!" McIntyre said, excitement in his voice.

I felt, more than saw, him sit down on the bed next to me.

I pulled myself up into a sitting position against the headboard and pillows, noticing Jeremy, Alex, and Braden for the first time. "Hi, guys."

They all gave me their well wishes and said how happy they were that I was home safely. Then they awkwardly made their escape into the hallway, leaving me alone with my Master. I motioned for the bottle of water that I saw on the nightstand, and he got it for me. The water tasted great on my chapped lips and my dry mouth.

"Master, I—"

He stopped me before I could say anything else. "Brand, I am the one that needs to apologize to you. It's my job as the Master to protect you, and I failed . . . miserably." His normally jovial smile was replaced with a hound dog expression and his pale gray eyes were dark under his protruding brow. "So I want to say I'm sorry, for what it's worth."

"Master, it wasn't your fault. It was those assholes . . ." I said a little too loudly.

"If you don't want Marsh to go through with the Master transfer tomorrow, I would understand." He almost choked on the words, hanging his head as he said them.

I reached over and lifted his chin. The tiny dark hairs of his unshaven face pricked my fingers and immediately sent a signal to my crotch to awaken.

"I would never want to belong to anyone but you, Master."

"Truly?" he asked in surprise.

"For sure, Master," I told him, unable to not smile. "Now, tell me all about what happened at the Shadow Ball after I was taken out."

Marshall Taylor stepped in my room, saying that the boys had told him that I was awake. He listened to Chase tell me all about how the rest of the charity event went down—how Ricky avoided him, how he knew right away that Ricky wasn't me, how he confronted him about being in on it, etc.

"What happened next, Master?" I asked, fascinated listening to his account of what had happened.

"He broke down under McIntyre's pressure," Marshall said proudly.

Chase picked up the story, saying, "He cried like a baby and said he was ordered by his Master. He wouldn't say who his Master was. I think he was more afraid of them than he was of me."

"I'll say. They were terrible to him, I think." I looked at McIntyre quizzically and asked, "Then how did you know where to find me, Master?"

McIntyre turned to Taylor and said, "Marsh had some contacts with The Service, and one of them let us swing by, even though it was the middle of the night."

"What did he do, Masters?"

Marshall said, "He had a scanner that ran Ricky's fingerprint and told us exactly who his Master was."

"Thank you, Masters," I said, bowing my head.

"I had to make sure you were safe, Brand."

"I'm very lucky to have both of you looking over me."

Marshall smiled and said, "Well, I'm going to go see what those three Servants of mine are up to . . ." He left the room with a wave.

I continued to try to put the pieces of this puzzle together in my head. "So, what happens to all those people now, Master?"

"Those asshole brother plumbers were arrested and will go to jail."

"They are all alive?"

"Yes, Brand. You didn't kill anyone."

"And Ricky? What will happen to him?"

"He probably got the best deal. His contract was voided, he was returned to The Service, and the brothers will have to pay him his share of the contract."

"That's good, Master."

McIntyre smirked at me for the first time since this whole ordeal. "Speaking of who has been good and who hasn't . . . we're going to need to discuss how bad you've been . . ."

"Me, Master?" I asked, shocked.

"Yes, you. You will have to be punished when you are feeling better."

I laughed out loud, glad to know it was a sexual thing and not something that I had really done to displease him. "How about now, Master?"

"No, you've been through an ordeal, and you need to rest."

"That's a shame," I said lustfully.

He narrowed his eyes at me, but his smirk changed to a face-splitting grin. "Don't test me," he grumbled.

"I so want to test you, Master, plus you haven't told me why you think I have been bad."

"Shall I count the ways?" He smirked. I nodded and he began to count on his fingers as he talked. "Well, first, you did not obey my direct order to come to me in the lounge after your time on the belt was over." I completely rolled my eyes. "Second, you have kept me from enjoying your particular . . . talents . . . for more than two days now."

"Master!" I said, exasperated with him.

He held a finger up to silence me. "Third, you have gone too long without being punished and fourth and fifth, that eye rolling of yours is in need of correction." He looked at me with a concerted nod of his head to let me know that he was entirely correct. "You may speak now."

"Well, I guess you have covered it all, Master. I desperately need to be punished."

"I thought so," he said with a smirk.

CHAPTER TWENTY-FIVE

The next morning, I was feeling like myself again and couldn't wait to see my Master. I was a little surprised he wasn't in the bed with me when I woke up, but I put it out of my mind, got dressed, and went down to the kitchen.

I walked into the kitchen and saw that Jeremy, Alex, and Braden were sitting at the counter. When they heard me come in, there was a universal spreading of a giant smile across their faces.

"What?" I asked with attitude.

"There's something here for you," Jeremy said, starting to laugh.

"What?" I repeated.

"Eat some breakfast and then we'll show you." Alex slid a plate with a waffle on it over to me.

I took a look at the plate and saw that it had waffles, bananas and walnuts on it, which were my favorites. "What is going on?"

"Eat," Braden said, passing me the syrup.

Sighing, knowing that they were not going to let me in on the joke, I decided to just eat and get caught up with my friends. They had a lot of things to tell me and I them.

"Where's the NOMARs?" I asked, stuffing waffle into my mouth.

"They went to practice. They will be back for the transfer."

When I was done eating, they were all smiles again. "What?"

"We think you should go to the living room," Jeremy said

suddenly.

"Subtle," Alex poked him.

I put my dishes in the sink and headed for the living room. All three boys followed me. When I turned the corner, I was shocked as hell to see a marked man sitting on the sofa. I walked around the second sofa and saw that it was Nathan, who had been my handler when I entered into Service.

A handler was a marked man who worked for The Service, getting Servants ready, answering questions, checking on their progress once placed, and locking them into the cage for the ultimate journey.

I was happy to see him and wrapped him in a big hug. "Nathan, what are you doing here? Are you here for the transfer of Masters?"

"Yes," he answered. "You know no one can do this for you but me," he said mysteriously.

"Do what?"

He looked behind the couch and I followed his gaze. It was my cage.

"No way," I said.

"Of course. You have to be delivered to your Master in your cage. You know the rules," Nathan said, like I was a petulant child who needed to be told the rules over and over.

"Yes, I know the rules. I just thought that . . ."

Nathan looked at me with just a hint of sympathy in his eyes and said, "You just thought you could fuck around with your new Master for a while this morning before the transfer?"

"Exactly!"

"Well, it's not going to happen, Brand." Nathan chuckled. "Strip."

"Right now?" I was surprised this was happening so fast.

"Yes."

"Brand, we have something for you on your big day!"

Jeremy said, practically yelling because he was so excited.

I turned around and saw that the three of them were grinning like fools, and stretched between their hands was the standard jock that all Servants wear. It looked very familiar, with the three elastic bands that would outline my ass and the small square of fabric in the front that would just barely cover my junk. What was not recognizable was the material. It looked like it was hand-made.

Making my way towards it, I saw that it was made out of Chase McIntyre's jersey. It had his number 44 on it and was the team's colors. I smiled broadly and said, "He's going to fucking love this. Thanks, guys!"

I stripped down, changed into the new jock, entered my cage, and settled in to wait. It was a small price to pay to be with this man whom I had come to feel was my whole world. Nathan drew the drapes around my cage, locked the padlock, and I settled in to see what was next.

What seemed to be at least two hours later, I heard the faint sounds of people coming into the living room. The curtain was muting most of the sound, so I reached between the bars, lifted up a section of the curtain closest to the couches and listened intently.

"Mac, sit here." It was Taylor's voice.

"So then you are ready to start, Mr. Taylor?" I didn't recognize this voice at all, but figured it had to be The Service lawyer.

"Shouldn't we go get Brand?" McIntyre asked.

"He's busy," Taylor said.

I smiled to myself inside the dark cage.

"Busy doing what?" McIntyre demanded.

I was happy to see my new Master being given some orders, for a change. I wasn't sure why no one answered him or if there was a non-verbal, but the lawyer began to go through the paperwork. It was a long tedious process that made me have new respect for the Masters that made the cut and for The Service for protecting us with so much paperwork.

After what seemed like an eternity in the hot cage, I heard Taylor's voice. "Well, if my part is over, I'm going to take my leave."

"Where are you going?" McIntyre asked.

"I'm taking my boys on a little road trip to the Finger Lakes."

"Overnight?"

"Yeah. Thought you could use the house tonight."

"Thanks, Marsh!" I could hear the excitement in Chase's voice and the joy of being his own Master, literally.

"You deserve it, Mac . . . and so does Brand."

The Service lawyer asked, "Would you like Brand's file, Mr. McIntyre?"

"No, thanks. I know everything about him that I need to."

"Very well."

With that, it got very quiet as my new Master signed the rest of the paperwork and finished the transfer.

"Very good. Well, congratulations, Mr. McIntyre, you are now the proud Master of a new Servant." Realizing a little too late that the lawyer was probably pointing at my cage, I hastily dropped the curtain and got into The Service Squat.

"Thanks so much," McIntyre said, and then there was a lull.

I wondered if he was showing the lawyer out. That was answered immediately for me when the drape was pulled back on the cage and I could see his feet on the carpet in front of me. He was, much to my shock, wearing expensive-looking dress shoes and jeans.

"Servant, I am your Master."

I didn't answer or look up. My heart was beating a thousand times a second and my legs felt like they would give out on me at any minute.

Master unlocked my cage and opened the door wide. "Come out so I can get a look at you." His voice was so deep and heady with lust and need that it didn't even sound like his. It did nothing but excite me even more, causing my cock to fill with blood and harden against my stomach. I crawled out of the cage and returned to The Squat.

"Look at me," he commanded.

I slowly lifted my head and drank him in with my gaze. His jeans were tailored for his big legs and fit perfectly. His dress shirt was also hand-made. McIntyre had a fresh-shorn face, and when our gazes met, I knew that everything I had dreamed of in my life up to this point had come true. He was the perfect man for me and I was the perfect man for him.

"You look good in that jersey," Master smirked.

"I've got something for you in this jersey, Master," I said, my voice dripping with lust.

He held up two fingers in front of his smirk.

Was that punishments? Why had he skipped one?

I decided to ask, even though I knew I shouldn't. "Why two, Master?"

"Now, it's three. You got number one when I saw you raising the curtain on your cage."

I lowered my head and knew in my heart that I was caught and that I would never be able to get away with anything with this man. I smiled to myself, knowing that it was just what I needed. "Yes, sir."

"Open."

I opened my mouth and he spit a gloriously large loogie into it.

"Show me," he commanded.

I pushed my tongue forward and showed him his spit on my tongue and lips.

"Who is your Master?"

"You are, Master."

"That's right. I am your Master."

"Yes, sir."

"You belong to me."

"Yes, sir." I saw the outline of his huge lap-hog making itself known in those jeans.

"You will do what I command you to do."

"Yes, sir."

"And if you do, you will make me happy."

"Yes, Master."

"And if you don't, you will make me punish you."

"Yes, sir."

McIntyre smiled that beautiful smile and added, "And that will make me even happier."

I couldn't help but grin like a fool when I said, "Yes, Master."

"Now, get upstairs and await your punishment."

"Yes, Sir!"

YOU MAY ALSO ENJOY THE FOLLOWING FROM EXTASY BOOKS INC:

Cageless in College Junior Year
Crawford Rhine

Excerpt

June had brought the end of school and the beginning of another summer in Charleston for me. I had just finished my second year at the University of North Carolina, having the most amazing sexual experience of my life.

Now I was supposed to go home for three months and live without it?

Marcus Battle had been my boyfriend since the first month of freshman year when the football team decided that I needed one of them to fuck me on a regular basis. I didn't like being told what to do, but at the same time, I was given free rein to choose any football player I wanted to date, so it was a win-win situation for me.

I was a marked man, in a literal sense. On my face was a bright blue mark running from my earlobe to my chin. The mark appeared on the exact minute of my birth on my thirteenth birthday. It signaled to the world that I was a man who was sexually attracted to men, and since our world only contained men, it was one big meat market for me.

My father had always taught me that our world contained more threats to me than pleasures and he had been correct. NOMARs, or non-marked men, made up about ninety-eight percent of the population, and since there were no women, they were constantly horny. Dad had taught me to fight and defend myself, but most importantly, he had taught me how to think quickly, react in advance, and how to quickly assess my surroundings for potential danger.

Fortunately for me, I had not run into any major problems. Once in high school, I found a popular senior to date who usually ran interference for me and kept trouble at bay. I did the same thing the next year and then the next and assumed that I would live my life that way. These men were easy to manipulate, and most of them bent to my will without even the flicker of fight in their eyes.

When I arrived on campus at UNC, I naturally thought it would be smart to find a protector, but I also let loose a little and fucked around with a lot of guys. By the time the football team offered me their protection, I was ready to see what came of it. Dating several of the older players, I found them lacking. Fortunately for me, I was intrigued by a quiet freshman and gave him a chance.

Marcus turned out to be the most amazing man I had ever met. He was not as susceptible to my charms as every other NOMAR I had met and refused to fuck me or even let me see his cock until I had committed to him. There was some kind of attraction between the two of us that I could not explain. I had never felt anything like it before, and I could not get enough of it.

It took two weeks for me to take the risk and accept Marcus as the football player that I wanted to date. He had been there when I needed him and I told him that I wanted him to be my boyfriend. He was excited, but still held out on sex until I informed the team of my decision.

When Marcus and I finally fucked, it was mind-blowing sex that I had never felt before. Marcus' cock was huge and he certainly knew how to use it, but the real fire came from the connection between us. We just couldn't get enough of each other, and therefore we had to set limits very quickly. Marcus and I were both excellent students and he also was a member of the football team, so we didn't want either of those two things to suffer just because we couldn't stay out of each other's pants.

We spent our first year together feeling each other out. Marcus demanded that I work out to be able to keep up with him, and I was more than willing. I didn't want anything to hold me back from being with him. Marcus and I had a great year together, and over the summer, he had told me to take an older lover to keep me out of trouble.

I had worked out a deal with the boss at my summer job at IBM that allowed him to fuck around with me in exchange for a summer job and the company scholarship each school year. Mr. Lewellyn, my boss, had taught me more than I bargained for. He was into bondage, and the things that he did to me, made me realize that I wanted to explore it with Marcus.

My chance to do just that came at the end of summer when I bound myself to Marcus' locker on the last day of football camp. He took total advantage of me and we wound up spending the rest of the summer together. It was such life-altering sex, but neither Marcus nor I were ready to fully realize what it meant.

Marcus Battle had started to make some noise on the football field in his second year and we both had matured physically in the year since we had met. Marcus had grown into a man and not an overgrown boy like before.

A spring break trip in our sophomore year to the Bahamas had sealed the connection for us. We both had enjoyed someone else's attention on that trip, but had come out of the other side to realize that we were what each of us needed. I had marked him as my man and he had marked me as his.

At the end of our second year, Marcus had snatched me from my final exam and taken me to a hotel room where he asserted his dominance over me. My footballer boyfriend had bound me, controlled me, forced me to address him as Master, and then given me the greatest sexual pleasure of my life.

That experience had happened a week ago. I was now at home in Charleston, and Marcus was at his father's home in Ohio. I thought back to it often.

ABOUT THE AUTHOR

Crawford Rhine is easily inspired by travelling. His series, The Romanian Chronicles, was inspired by a summer trip to Romania and Russia where he completed four books and has added some since. These books are re-imaginings of the classic movie monsters from the 1930's, updated with new twists like Dracula, Frankenstein, the Werewolf, and the Phantom of the Opera. A recent trip to Switzerland provides the backdrop for the Invisible Man, still to be published.

Crawford's first series The Master & Servant Series are inspired by sports and occupations that traditionally exude masculinity like baseball, basketball, football, acting, and being a country music star. A trip to Denmark has inspired a book on soccer still to come.

He looks forward to continuing to travel to far-away places and publishing more books in each series.